A Deal with a

HISTORICAL REGENCY ROMANCE NOVEL

Dorothy Sheldon

Table of Contents

Chapter One...3

Chapter Two 9

Chapter Three..17

Chapter Four..25

Chapter Five...33

Chapter Six...41

Chapter Seven..49

Chapter Eight 56

Chapter Nine..61

Chapter Ten 70

Chapter Eleven...77

Chapter Twelve...83

Chapter Thirteen..90

Chapter Fourteen 97

Chapter Fifteen...104

Chapter Sixteen 111

Chapter Seventeen 117

Chapter Eighteen 123

Chapter Nineteen 130

Chapter Twenty 137

Chapter Twenty-One 144

Chapter Twenty-Two 151

Chapter Twenty-Three..157

Chapter Twenty-Four..164

Epilogue 171

Extended Epilogue 176

Chapter One

Lord and Lady Worthington had thrown a ball of jaw-dropping splendour. Of course, one would expect no less – it was the *first* ball of the Season, and so had to be truly spectacular.

The food was spread out on long tables, the finest and most exquisite dishes, and there was a seemingly endless supply of good wine, champagne, and punch to keep the dancers going.

Indeed, for this esteemed gathering was a splendid ball, wherein all those of noble standing were expected to partake in the merriment of dance.

Even, to her chagrin, Ava.

"... and there is the most subtle difference in floral scent, Lady Ava, and..."

"But they are both pink, aren't they? The roses, I mean." Ava interrupted and received a look of firm disapproval from her dance partner.

The man in question was Lord Alexander Pole, a rotund, red-haired young man, who had spent the entirety of the dance telling Ava about two types of rose he had bred himself, and the key differences between them. Ava was not particularly interested in flowers and gardening, but Lord Alexander did not seem to care. As far as she could tell, the roses were identical. She thoroughly regretted briefly complimenting the flower displays on the Worthingtons' mantelpiece, which had set off this nonsense altogether.

"Yes, Lady Ava, but that is not important." Lord Alexander said firmly.

"Well, I myself am not much of a gardener." Ava said hastily, hoping to steer the conversation in a different direction. "Although I do find natural science truly fascinating. There is a paper published recently..."

"Oh, no, I don't concern myself with that sort of thing." Lord Alexander interrupted, in a tone that indicated the subject would not be continued. "I must say, I am surprised to find that a lady of your standing would trouble herself with such nonsense. Do your parents allow it?"

Mercifully for Lord Alexander, the music stopped, and the

dance ended with a flourish. The dancers stepped apart from each other, bowed, then burst into applause and laughter.

Everyone, it seemed, had had a good time except for Ava. Quietly seething, she flashed Lord Alexander a smile and turned to leave the dance floor.

Clearly disregarding the insinuation, the gentleman hastened to her vicinity.

"Pray, may I procure for you a cup of punch, Lady Ava?"

"I am afraid I must seek out my family." She said as lightly as she could. "I think my sister will be looking for me. This is her first ball, you see, and she's rather nervous."

The moment she closed her mouth, Ava wished she hadn't been so foolish as to let that detail slip. Lord Alexander pursed his lips.

"Your sister, Lady Ava? Your *younger* sister?"

Curses, she thought, but of course it was too late to avoid this now.

"Yes." She said, trying to sound as if it were nothing of consequence. "My sister, Lady Suzanne, comes out this Season."

"But you are not married. I thought it was not proper for a younger sister to come out when her older sister is not married."

Ava was thoroughly glad that she did not have a cup of anything in her hand, because she certainly would have tossed it in his face.

Instead, she gave a wide, brilliant smile.

"Oh, it is not, Lord Alexander. However, I am twenty-six years old and my sister is very nearly eighteen, so it seems a little unfair for her to miss out on her share of life, don't you think, simply because I choose not to marry?"

"*Choose?*" he echoed, faintly scandalized.

"I believe a younger sister coming out is viewed in the same light as a lady choosing to study mathematics, natural history, archaeology, and the sciences. It is disapproved of, but really, nobody can stop me. Good day to you, Lord Alexander."

She turned on her heel and marched off into the crowd without another word. She was reasonably certain that he would not follow her, and he didn't. With a sigh of relief, Ava spotted a familiar flame-red head above the crowd and headed towards it.

"*There* you are, Willi." Ava complained, pushing her way

4

through the last of the crowd to join her friend in a quiet corner. "I didn't see you dancing."

"Oh, I opted to abstain from partaking in this particular dance." Willi said, with a tinge of regret. Miss Wilhelmina Trent, known affectionately to her friends as *Willi*, was blessed with rich, adoring parents, a fine character, a sharp mind, and a truly charming personality.

She was not, however, blessed with looks. Her bright red hair, which Ava thought was truly spectacular, was generally disapproved of for some reason. She had large blue eyes, hidden by round, wire-rimmed spectacles, and a round, good-natured face. Besides the pampered, powdered beauties of the Season, Willi looked like a peahen beside peacocks, a state of affairs which infuriated Ava.

More often than not, gentlemen approaching the pair of them would glance over Willi without a second look and settle hopefully on Ava.

Ava knew, in a disinterested sort of way, that she was beautiful. She had olive skin, large hazel eyes, good features, and a head of glossy black hair. She had been described as having *spirit*, whatever that meant, and gentlemen seemed to like that.

She had no patience with any of them. They were all senseless imbeciles, every single one, looking for a pretty woman to bear a few suitable heirs and spend her life sitting docilely in a parlour while he entertained his friends.

Willi leaned against the wall and sipped her champagne, eyeing Ava thoughtfully.

"I saw you marching away from Lord Alexander Pole as if he'd offended you. Care to explain?"

Ava huffed. "Well, he *had*. You should have heard him, you know. He talked about two identical types of roses during our dance. During the whole dance, Willi! I don't mind listening to a man's interests, of course not, but the second I tried to mention natural history and Doctor Armitage's paper, he simply…"

"Oh, *Ava*! You mustn't talk like that. Gentlemen don't like ladies to be cleverer than them."

She rolled her eyes. "That's unfortunate, since you, at least, are cleverer than every single man in this room."

Willi sighed. "Perhaps so, but bluestockings don't do well in

5

Society. You are lucky — stricter parents than dear Lord and Lady Mortensen would not allow you to study the way you do."

Ava flinched at that. It was an unpleasant reminder that at twenty-six, she was still little more than a child, living on the good graces of her parents. Ava had no money of her own and would not receive any until she married. Oh, her parents loved her, of course, and gave her a generous allowance, but that was not *her* money. She studied whatever subjects caught her interest, but at the back of her mind was the knowledge that her father could choose to stop her at any moment and would be well within his legal rights to do so.

She had told Lord Alexander that nobody could stop her in her studies, but of course, for a woman, that was not true.

He wouldn't, of course. but he *could*, and that grated. A gentleman of twenty-six, in contrast, was a grown man with all the freedoms he could desire. It was not *fair*.

"Kind of you to remind me." Ava muttered.

Willi shook her head. "I'm not being unkind, Ava. You really need to be serious now that Suzi has come out. There's lots of gossip about you already. You're twenty-six, and every gentleman who has shown an interest in you has been firmly turned away. You must start thinking of a husband. If Suzi is married before you, you'll be the laughingstock of London."

"I don't care!" Ava said fiercely, her raised voice almost pitching above the babble and chatter of the crowd. A few inquiring glances were shot their way, and she composed herself as best she could. "I don't care, Willi. Don't you see that marriage would be the end of everything for me? The end of my freedom, such as it is, the end of my studies... no, I can't consider it. I hope Suzi finds a suitable man, as I know she wants to get married, but for myself, I'd like to go on as I am."

"Ava..."

"I think I need a breath of fresh air, Willi. Do you have a partner for the next dance?"

"I do." Willi responded unwillingly, glancing towards the dance floor.

"Well, you'd better stay here, then."

"Where are you going?"

"I want to *breathe*, Willi." Ava responded, already slipping away into the crowd. She shot her friend one last lopsided grin over her shoulder and headed towards the terraces.

In the interests of getting air into the stuffy ballroom, their hosts had thrown open the wide French doors leading out onto the balcony. Steps led down from the balcony onto the terrace below, and from there into the dark garden. Footmen were posted on the terrace, to discreetly but firmly turn away any guests from wandering in the gardens. After all, if an unchaperoned couple were to find themselves in the garden, their reputation would be destroyed. The Worthington family would also suffer, since the scandal would have happened at *their* ball.

It was all ridiculous. Ava shouldn't have stepped onto the balcony alone, but she really did need some air. There were a cluster of ladies on the balcony, none of them above eighteen, leaning on the stone parapet and giggling madly among themselves. They glanced over at Ava, glanced at each other, then dissolved into further giggles.

Rolling her eyes, Ava turned towards the stone staircase. She would go down to the terrace and think about the book she sadly left at home. She would have finished it by now if she'd been permitted to skip the first ball of the Season.

Lost in her contemplations, Ava did not pay attention to where she was putting her feet. The second to last stone stair was a little mossy, slick with the recent rain, and her flat-soled dancing slippers had no grip to speak of at all. Without warning, her foot skidded out from under her, and Ava tipped forward towards the shadowy terrace, her arms flailing like the sails of a windmill.

She hit something soft and firm, that gave a muffled *oof*. A strong pair of arms steadied her, large hands gripping her upper arms and setting her squarely on her feet as if she weighed very little at all.

Ava blinked and found herself looking up at a strange man to whom she had not been introduced. He wore a deep green evening suit, a rather carelessly tied cravat, and had sandy blond hair which stuck up as if he'd been running his fingers through it.

"Do forgive me, madam." He said, and his voice was deep and unfamiliar. He removed his hands from her arms, and Ava cleared her throat, recovering herself.

"Not at all, sir. The fault was mine. Thank you for your help."

He bowed wordlessly, and climbed up the stone stairs to the balcony, leaving Ava alone.

Chapter Two

"You smoke too much, Dominic."

Dominic flinched, glancing guiltily over his shoulder, and tapped out the contents of his pipe against the wall.

His friend, Lord Richard Forbury, Viscount of Larchmere, was watching him from the shadows, arms crossed, face disapproving.

"A man can have his small comforts, can he not?" Dominic responded mildly. "I cannot indulge in tobacco within the premises. The young ones persistently seek my attention, preventing me from partaking and Daniella has recently taken an aversion to pipe smoke."

Richard pursed his lips, unconvinced.

Lord Larchmere was something of an enigma, if the scandal sheets were to be believed. He had the look of a libertine – a cherubic face that would make any woman swoon, chestnut brown curls that Lord Byron himself would have envied, and a figure that most men aspired to attain through the use of padding and the wearing of corsets.

And then Lord Larchmere went and ruined it all by acting like a prissy matron. He did not smoke, drink, gamble, or waltz, if he could help it. He had been described by one particular scandal sheet as a man entirely without vices or fault.

That was an odd way of describing a person, Dominic had always thought. *Without vices*. He himself did not have *time* for vices. Raising three children did not leave much time for anything, let alone vice.

"What about you, Richard? Have any of the mammas in there got you married off, yet?"

Richard scowled, an expression which made his beautiful face look even more beautiful, somehow. Dominic, who was aware he looked tired and sallow after staying up to manage Steven's nightmares the previous night, felt an unfamiliar pang of envy. Richard was twenty-eight, barely two years younger than his friend, and already Dominic felt like an old man whose life was slipping away.

"I will marry if and when I choose." Richard said shortly.

"Charming. Save it for the ladies, please."

9

Richard rolled his eyes, leaning against the wall and staring out at the garden. "What about you, Dom? Have you found any suitable matrons to raise your children yet?"

"I wish you wouldn't say it like that. It makes me sound terrible. And the answer is no, I have not."

"Really? In this crowd of eager young ladies, all longing to be married and have a family of their own, you haven't found a single one who likes children?"

Dominic pressed his lips together. "It's a great deal more complicated than that, Richard, and you know it. It is not a matter of merely discovering a lady who possesses an affinity towards children. I need a woman of good character, of strength and intelligence. I want a partner, not a nursemaid. I can hire a nursemaid. First of all, I'm ruling out all the debutantes, as they're entirely too young. I don't want some eighteen- or twenty-one-year-old girl trying to mother my children. They ought to be building their own lives, not helping a sad widower piece together his own. And the children deserve better."

There was a silence after that, and Dominic bit his lip, wishing he'd stayed quiet.

"You are too hard on yourself, you know." Richard said quietly. "You're a good man, and the children are sweet."

Dominic swallowed hard past the lump in his throat, raking a hand through his hair. He didn't look at Richard, preferring instead to stare at the dark shapes in the garden, trying to work out what they might be. Rose bushes, or shrubberies?

He hoped the latter. He hated roses.

"It's been close to two years since Marianne died." He said softly. "And I still feel her absence every day. Is it right for me to marry now, Richard? Is it wise? Wouldn't I be condemning some poor woman to a life of second best? I loved Marianne, and I never thought..." he trailed off, shaking his head.

Richard shifted beside him, sighing. He was trying his best, Dominic knew, but Richard had never been comfortable with excesses of emotion, despite his best efforts.

"Marianne told you, on her deathbed, that you should marry again, did she not?" he said, after a pause. "She told you to love again, to find somebody to mother the children. She didn't tell you when. If you truly feel that you aren't ready to marry again, then we can go home, you and I, right now. I have my carriage, and we can both drop out of the Season whenever you like. There need be no pressure."

Dominic closed his eyes, letting his head sink back against the stone wall. It was an appealing thought, just going home and forgetting the business of the Season, of socialising, of finding a woman to marry and share his life.

He wasn't looking for love, of course. Marianne had wanted him to fall in love again, but Dominic did not expect that. He was looking for a woman who would suit him and his family, and they would suit her. He wanted a marriage of convenience for them both, and that seemed almost more difficult than simply charming some young woman. Simply wooing a woman felt like *deceit*, somehow.

"I have procrastinated upon it for an extended period, but I believe the time has arrived for me to broach this matter." Dominic finally voiced his thoughts. "Emily, the governess – she has been an absolute blessing. The children adore her, and she *knew* Marianne so well. But Emily is getting older, and it's not fair to make her manage three growing children. Especially with Daniella's behaviour at the moment, it's simply... it's simply too much. Now is the time, Richard. I'm determined to find a wife this Season."

Richard nodded. "As you like." He paused, tilting his head, listening to the strains of music starting up from inside the house. "Oh, dear. The next set is starting."

"Oh, have you a partner?" Dominic asked, teasingly. "Has the aloof Lord Larchmere finally lowered himself to ask a woman to dance?"

Richard scowled. "I'm dancing with Lady Worthington's daughter. She's my host, I have to ask her to dance. But don't worry – Miss Worthington prefers heroic, grizzled soldiers and is all but engaged to one of them. I'm quite safe."

Dominic chuckled. "*Quite safe.*" He muttered to himself, eyeing Richard's retreating back.

He was sure that Richard secretly wished to be married – why else would he attend all of the Seasons? – but whatever type of woman he was searching for, he had not found her.

Richard had been gone for a moment or two when another figure appeared at the top of the stairs, a dark-haired woman in a blue dress. Dominic glanced up at her and did not recognize her. There were plenty of people at the party he had not been introduced to, and he was more than happy to keep it that way. The woman began to descend the stairs. No doubt she'd come out here for a breath of fresh air and couldn't have seen him in the shadows.

He would have to leave, of course, as it wouldn't be proper to stand out here together, even if they never exchanged a single word. Dominic pushed away from the wall, feeling the familiar twinge of annoyance at Society's ridiculous rules and proprieties.

Then the woman's foot slipped on a step, and she went hurtling forward. Dominic dived forward without even thinking about it, neatly catching her in his arms. He set her down on her feet and eyed her for any signs of damage. She seemed shaken – a fall of only two steps from the bottom was still a long way, as those stairs were steep – but in no danger of swooning anytime soon.

She was remarkably pretty, with olive-tinged skin and a straightforward, clear hazel gaze. She met his eye squarely, with none of the demurring or downcast eyes that ladies favoured these days. Dominic realized that he had his hands still resting on her arms, and hastily removed them.

"Do forgive me, madam." He said, taking a polite step backwards.

She seemed to recover herself, flashing a quick, tight-lipped smile.

"Not at all, sir. The fault was mine. Thank you for your help."

And so it was concluded. Dominic bowed, and began to climb the stairs, to reassure her that he did not intend to linger on the terrace and endanger her reputation. He glanced back once over his shoulder and saw that she was now standing where he had stood, leaning back against the wall, staring out into the garden. She looked pensive, and her dark brows knitted over her eyes.

Sighing, Dominic continued up the stairs, past a gaggle of debutantes, and back into the sticky heat of the ballroom.

The dance was in full swing. Picking up a glass of wine, Dominic leaned against the mantelpiece and watched the dancers. He was fond of dancing, and Marianne had been, too. Once the children began to come along, there'd been no time for balls and parties, of course. Still, every now and then, Marianne enlisted the long-suffering Emily to play the piano, and Dominic and she moved the furniture in the drawing room and danced a few giddy, lopsided measures together.

He swallowed hard, the laughter in his head dying away.

Maybe I should ask somebody to dance.

"Ah, there you are, Lord Thame."

Dominic stiffened, cursing himself for a fool. He'd let his guard drop, and now Mrs Ursula Winslow had cornered him.

Ursula was perhaps twenty-six or twenty-seven and had already secured herself the reputation as a Dashing Widow. She was tall, slim, and fashionably fair, with a face like a doll and a fascinating pair of brown eyes. She was out of mourning now, of course – and everyone knew how keen she was to throw off her black satins and silks – and was generally said to be on the lookout for another husband.

She settled herself beside Dominic, leaning against the mantelpiece.

"Mrs Winslow, good evening." Dominic responded politely. "Are you not dancing?"

"Not this time. Why, are you asking?"

He swallowed hard. "I think it is too late. The dance has already begun."

Ursula nodded slowly, lifting a glass of champagne to her lips. She eyed him closely – *she* didn't drop her gaze demurely, either – and there was a calculating gleam in her eye which he did not like.

"How are you dear children, Lord Thame?" she asked suddenly. "Daniella, Steven, and Margaret?"

He gave a tight smile. "Maria. The youngest is named Maria."

She winced, shaking her head as if she'd been caught using the wrong fork at a dinner. "Ah, I beg your pardon. You have yet to introduce me to your children, you know, Lord Thame. You know how I adore children."

"Yes, Mrs Winslow, you have mentioned it. I'm sure you can meet them sometime. Unfortunately, events like this are simply not suitable for children."

She blinked. "Why not?"

Dominic glanced down at her, not entirely sure whether she was serious or not. "Well, it's… it's too loud, and too late for them."

She smiled charmingly. "Of course, of course. Well, you shall simply have to invite me to your home then, won't you?"

He swallowed. This sounded suspiciously like he was being trapped into an invitation.

He was saved by the dance ending. Everyone around them broke out into applause, laughing and chattering. The musicians took a short break, tuning up their instruments and muttering between themselves, while the dancers filed off the dance floor, aiming for the refreshment tables.

Richard appeared, and Dominic sagged in relief. Ursula eyed him, flashing a smile which did not reach her eyes. Richard bowed, blank-faced, and said nothing.

"Well, I had better take myself off." Ursula said brightly. "Good day, gentlemen."

She glided off into the crowd, throwing one calculating glance back at the two men. Dominic let out a sigh of relief, draining his glass of wine.

Richard pursed his lips, folding his arms.

"She'd marry you in a heartbeat."

"Yes, I know, Richard. She's made that quite clear. She keeps telling me how much she loves children."

Richard lifted an eyebrow. "And yet you aren't keen. Why not?"

"Why not? Why *not*? You can't stand the woman yourself, Richard."

His friend shook his head. "That's different."

"How is it different?"

"I am not looking for a woman to raise my children. Mrs Winslow is… well, she's a very calculating woman. She all but tricked her late husband into marrying her, and if rumours are to be believed, she ruined at least two innocent young women in her path to marrying the man. Now she's widowed and free again, and she's looking for another rich man – a younger and handsomer one, this time. But she has no children, so perhaps she wants a family, too."

14

Dominic sighed. "There's something about her that I don't like. Something cold. I'm not marrying for my own sake, Richard. Of course, I want to *like* the woman I marry, but my children need to like her, too. It feels like an impossible task at times. Besides, there's no guarantee we would have more children. I need to marry a woman who'll love my children as her own, and if we *did* have more children, she could not make a divide between them. A great deal rests on this."

Richard nodded but said nothing. For a moment or two, they simply stood together, watching the crowd.

A twinge ran down Dominic's spine when he saw a familiar face enter from the balcony. The woman who'd fallen into him, with her olive skin and dark hair.

She moved easily through the crowd, smiling at a few acquaintances, until she came to a knot of three people. One was a red-haired, bespectacled young woman, and the other two were clearly the woman's siblings. One was a man, with the same dark hair and olive skin, and the other was a young lady of about seventeen, dressed like a debutante, and clearly simmering with nerves.

He watched the young girl's face light up at the sight of her sister, and he saw the woman smile warmly back at her. Conversation flowed between the four of them, and it was clear that they were all enjoying each other's company.

The debutante kept her eyes on her older sister's face, with something akin to adoration. They talked and laughed for a moment more, and Dominic noticed that the red-haired young lady, despite being the only one there not blood related (he guessed) did not seem excluded in the least.

"Richard." Dominic said suddenly, making his friend jump, "Who is that young woman?"

He pointed, and Richard squinted. "Which one? There are three."

"All of them, then."

"Well, the gentleman is Lord Gordon Devane, the red-haired lady is Miss Trent, if I'm not mistaken. The debutante is Lady Suzanne Devane, and the older woman is Lady Ava Devane. The Devanes are the children of Lord and Lady Mortensen."

"Oh, Richard! It appears you've consumed every tome of The

Spectator that exists. Might you kindly make the acquaintance for me?"

Richard let out a breath. "Which one do you want introducing to?"

"All of them, I suppose."

"You know what I mean."

Dominic pursed his lips, avoiding his friend's incisive stare. "The older Lady Devane."

"Lady Ava? Well, if you like."

"Are you a friend of the family?"

"No, but I make it my business to know everyone. It's a tedious job, however, it proves advantageous on certain occasions."

Richard seemed to be waiting for another question. Dominic shifted from foot to foot before he managed it.

"Are any of the ladies attached?" he asked lightly, deliberately not specifying. Richard rolled his eyes.

"Miss Trent is not, Lady Suzanne is not, having only just come out, and neither is Lady Ava. Why do you want to be introduced to her?"

Dominic considered making a joke or making a demurral. He was still watching Lady Ava, who was assiduously straightening her sister's necklace with an expression of absolute absorption. Her sister was still looking up at her with adoration, and it made something in Dominic's chest clench. He knew nothing at all about Lady Ava, aside from her name and the fact she was the kind of woman who'd stand alone on a terrace.

"Because." Dominic said, a little shocked at how tremulous and nervous his own voice sounded, "I want to ask her to dance with me."

16

Chapter Three

Ava was so focused on rearranging Suzi's necklace – a lovely gold chain with a diamond pendant, bought especially for her first ever ball in real Society – that she didn't notice the two approaching men until Gordon stiffened and nudged her, digging a sharp elbow into her ribs.

"Lord Larchmere, Lord Thame." He said, in the light, airy voice he thought made him sound very languid and grown-up. Gordon might have been twenty-eight, but he sometimes acted as if he were eighteen.

Ava stopped fidgeting with the necklace, seeing how crimson Suzi had gone – a sure sign that attractive gentlemen were approaching. She turned to see a vaguely familiar gentleman, remarkably handsome but with a severe expression, and the same fair-haired gentleman who'd saved her from falling down the stone stairs.

There was a taut moment of uncomfortable silence.

"Lord Devane, let me introduce my friend, Lord Dominic Broughton, the Marquess of Thame." The handsome gentleman intoned – Ava's memory supplied that his name was Lord Richard Forbury, Viscount of Larchmere – and gestured to his companion. "Lord Thame, this is Lord Gordon Devane, his sisters Lady Ava and Lady Suzanne, and their companion Miss Wilhelmina Trent."

Pleasantries and such were exchanged, and there was a half-minute of awkward silence. Lord Larchmere appeared wholly disinclined to engage in conversation.

Lord Thame cleared his throat and spoke first.

"Lady Ava, I was wondering if you'd care to stand up with me for the next dance? If you do not already have a partner, of course."

More silence. Ava glanced around at the others. Lord Larchmere's face was entirely impassive – now that she remembered his name, she remembered the various nicknames ascribed to him – Lord Ice, the Marble Gentleman, and even Matron Larchmere for his severity – while Willi and Suzi looked thrilled. Gordon looked faintly amused.

Well, it wasn't as if she could refuse. Declining an invitation

17

to dance was deemed highly inappropriate, and Ava would be unable to accept an invitation to dance for the rest of the evening, which would doubtless stretch out for hours and hours. This was Suzi's first ever ball, and Ava had no expectation of their family rushing home early, if they could help it. No, this party was for *Suzi*, and even if Lord Thame had been the most annoying gentleman in the world, she would not have embarrassed her sister by refusing his invitation.

"Of course." she said, with a practised smile. "I should love to. Shall we take our places?"

Lord Thame weaved his way through the crowd towards the dance floor, where other couples were already taking their places. Ava followed, mind reeling. Had he come over to scold her for walking unchaperoned on the terrace? No, he wouldn't have done so on the dance floor. He couldn't possibly have had an interest piqued in her from *that* altercation. With a jolt, Ava realized that the dance was...

"This is a waltz." She burst out, before she could stop herself.

Lord Thame hesitated, on the edge of the ballroom. "Yes, it is. I don't believe that our hosts prohibit the waltz between unmarried couples who are not engaged. We are all welcome to dance the waltz. Do you have any reservations about participating in the waltz? I would detest causing you any unease."

He would hate to make me uncomfortable, Ava thought, with a sudden rush of bitterness. *Because I am a staid old spinster who is shocked at the thought of a waltz.*

She'd already seen Suzi stand up for *two* waltzes with two different gentlemen, and *she* seemed entirely unaffected. She even seemed to enjoy the dance, claiming that it was simpler than other complex dances, which were faster and more energetic.

Lord Thame was still looking at her, waiting patiently for her response.

"I have no objection to the waltz." Ava heard herself say. "I don't often dance the waltz, however."

How about never?

"Neither do I." Lord Thame admitted, smiling wryly. "We can fumble through the steps together, I suppose. Shall we?"

There was nothing left now but to take her place on the

dance floor. Ava had, of course, learned the waltz along with her sisters – and Gordon, who was a remarkably graceful dancer – and she knew the steps well enough.

The issue with the waltz, in Ava's opinion, was that it was entirely too close. In the other dances, a lady could distance herself from her partner. Except for a few twirls and some promenading, the steps were all one's own. In a waltz, two dancers became one creature, standing close enough to shock the more proper ladies and gentlemen of Society, whirling round and round the dance floor with nothing to look at but each other.

While the prohibition on waltzing had been lifted in all but the most austere of homes, some hosts still did not allow unmarried and unengaged couples to participate. Ava was entirely comfortable with this.

Lord Thame held his hand out to her, and there was nothing for it but to go to him. She rested her hand gingerly on his shoulder – broad, without any need for padding, she noticed – and tried not to think about his hand on her waist.

Cease this nonsense, she chided herself. You have only encountered this gentleman for a mere couple of minutes. Deny yourself from succumbing to an infatuation over his comely countenance. You are not Emily St Aubert, as portrayed in that abhorrent novel, fainting and swooning without control.

"Are you sure you are not uncomfortable?" Lord Thame said, breaking into her thoughts.

She levelled a blank stare at him. "You must think me a fragile creature, Lord Thame, to be undone by a simple dance."

He didn't flinch, as other gentlemen might have done at her sharp tone. Instead, he smiled wryly.

"I don't think you're a fragile creature at all, Lady Ava. Quite the opposite."

Before Ava could question him further on that statement, the music began.

The waltz was not a *slow* dance, but it certainly allowed the dancers to catch their breath more frequently and allowed for much more extensive conversation.

Even so, Ava stayed quiet for the first few minutes, concentrating on getting the steps right and not treading on Lord Thame's highly polished hessians.

She didn't allow herself to think about the foolishness of wearing *boots*, let alone *hessians*, to a ball.

"I hope you didn't mind my introducing myself in that way." Lord Thame said eventually. "Have you been invigorated by your time upon the terrace?"

Ah, so he *was* going to mention their unusual meeting.

"Quite refreshed, thank you." she responded smoothly. "Are you enjoying yourself?"

"Very much, thank you."

She snorted. "That is the wrong answer."

He lifted an eyebrow. "Consider my curiosity piqued. What would the right answer be, then?"

"Well, since this is *fashionable* Society, and it is never fashionable to be happy or content, you ought to have said something polite about the decorations but hinted that you were terribly bored. It's fashionable to be bored, you see."

"How intriguing. Are *you* bored, Lady Ava?"

"I am neither bored nor fashionable, I am afraid. It's an entertaining party, and our hosts have put a great deal of effort into it."

"I agree."

The dance called for the gentlemen to spin their partners around nimbly, and they did so. When the dance allowed for it, Lord Thame spoke again.

"I hear that your younger sister has just come out."

Her mouth tightened. "Are you going to comment on how she is out when I am not married?"

Lord Thame blinked, looking baffled. "What? No, I was not. I was only going to ask her age. She seems young."

"She is not eighteen. *Very* young." Ava said pointedly. A seventeen-year-old girl marrying a man of thirty would not cause a blink in Society, but Ava did not like to see those age gaps. She'd seen too many sixteen- or seventeen-year-old girls marry men of thirty, forty, even fifty and have it called a *good match*, but Ava strongly disagreed.

"She seems to be enjoying herself very much." Lord Thame continued, blithely unaware. "She seems nervous, which is to be expected. It is good that she has you here. It is clear that she adores you, her older sister."

Ava hadn't been expecting that. She blinked, a little taken aback.

"Well, I do my best. I am nearly eight years older than her, so I suppose I've always seen her as a child. She hates that, of course."

Lord Thame smiled wryly. "I can imagine. My oldest daughter is nearly eight years old, and fancies herself quite grown up."

Ava blinked, nearly missing a step. Children. He had children. Why was he asking her to waltz, when he had children and doubtless a spouse floating about somewhere in the crowd?

"Then I am surprised you are not dancing with your wife, Lord Thame." Ava said, more sharply than she'd intended. It didn't matter if he was married, of course, or at least it *shouldn't*. She was not interested in him, or in any man. She *wasn't*.

Lord Thame's expression froze for a moment. At first, Ava thought it was guilt, or frustration at letting his guard slip, but then she saw something tight and pained in his eyes.

"I am a widower, Lady Ava. I have been for two years."

There was a heartbeat of silence.

You fool, Ava, she scolded herself. *You assumed the worst, and now you've insulted and offended a man who is clearly mourning his wife.*

"Forgive me, I..." she began, but he shook his head, cutting her off.

"What was it you said to me earlier? There is nothing to forgive, the fault is mine. I assumed you knew I was a widower, which I should not have done. I have three children, in fact, and the youngest is only three years old. It's a difficult task, and I find my social graces lacking these days, whenever I venture from my house."

She chuckled lightly. "I think you are doing very well, Lord Thame. I am about to become Aunt Ava, which is tremendously exciting. My elder sister is expecting a child, and we're all thrilled, as you can imagine."

Lord Thame smiled. It was a proper smile, not a tight, polite Society grimace, and Ava was surprised to feel her heart thud harder in his chest. His smile showed even, white teeth, creasing up his eyes and making his face look warmer and *different*, somehow. It was gone as soon as it had arrived, and she found herself wanting him to smile again.

"Yes, waiting for a child is an exciting prospect. Are you parents looking forward to being grandparents?"

"Oh, very much so. They're taking all of the toys my siblings and I had when we were young and having them repainted and spruced up for the new baby. I have been suggesting that my sister name the baby after me, if it is a girl, but shockingly, they are refusing."

He chuckled, and Ava allowed herself a small smile at that. It was always pleasant to make somebody laugh.

"What are the names of your children?" she asked, feeling like it was the right question to ask.

He beamed. "Daniella is the eldest – the nearly-eight-year-old who fancies herself grown up. Steven is five years old, the only boy. He's remarkably serious, and very clever. Maria is three, the baby, and I would venture the best behaved out of them all. Raising children is horrifyingly difficult, in case nobody has told you. Nursemaids or not."

"They sound delightful. Is it difficult, raising them alone? Since you are... ahem. A widower."

Lord Thame didn't seem to take offence at her clumsy question. He eyed her with a strange expression for a minute or two, until Ava started to think that she had made a mistake.

"Is it difficult." He said at last. "Very difficult, especially without my dear wife at my side. I feel her absence every day, which provides another challenge, as I'm sure you can imagine. I adore my children, and it's important to me that they have the finest childhood I can provide. Unfortunately, that requires more than just education and comforts. Children are complex, and they are all different. It is by far the hardest challenge I have ever faced."

In the face of this outpouring, Ava wasn't sure what to do. She didn't believe for one moment that Lord Thame told every stranger he met about the difficulties of raising his children and how much he missed his wife. So why was he telling *her*?

She was saved from the awkwardness of making an unsatisfactory reply by the dance ending.

The music finished with a flourish, the dancers bowed to

each other, and the crowd broke out into applause. Ava clapped along with them, feeling bemused. How had the dance gone by so quickly? The sets always seemed interminably long, but dancing with Lord Thame – well, it hadn't been a *trial*, not in the slightest.

She flashed a hesitant smile up at him, wondering what to do next. Usually, at this point of a dance, she would be plotting how to escape her partner. She hadn't made any plots so far.

Lord Thame spoke up.

"I find myself quite parched. May I entice you to partake in a beverage? The refreshment table is over there.. Would you care for a tumbler of punch?"

"Are you fond of gardening, Lord Thame?" Ava heard herself say.

He blinked. "I... not particularly. I enjoy a pleasant garden, of course, but I'm not talented when it comes to gardening. Why do you ask?"

"My last dance partner talked to me about roses for twenty minutes. I'm not sure I can bear a repeat."

He chuckled, offering her his arm. "If I promise not to talk about flowers, will you come with me?"

"I don't see why not." Ava responded, taking his arm. Her fingers accidentally brushed the inch of bare skin at his wrist, and the contact sent tingles along Ava's arm. She swallowed hard and tried her level best to ignore it.

"Well, I've bored you with tales of *my* family for at least ten minutes." Lord Thame said, sipping his punch. "It's your turn, I think."

Ava sighed, draining her own tumbler of punch. She'd drank it too quickly and was beginning to feel pleasantly light-headed.

"Oh, there is not much of consequence to relate. I am fortunate to possess a commendable family, and my affection for them knows no bounds. The oldest of us all is my sister, Lady Beverley Connor, the one who is expecting a baby, and the only one of us all who is married. Then comes Gordon, then me, then Suzi. Lady Suzanne, I mean. Out of them all, I'm the only shocking one."

He lifted one sandy eyebrow, in a gesture that was making Ava feel dizzy for some reason.

"Shocking? How so?"

"Are you fond of natural history, Lord Thame?"

"Very much so. Why do you ask?"

She set down her empty cup, resisting the urge to pick up another. She'd had quite enough, so far.

"I am also fond of natural history. And mathematics, and literature, and many more subjects that are entirely unsuitable for a lady. Shocking, is it not?"

Lord Thame chuckled, shaking his head. "I can imagine that Society is quiet scandalized. Foolishness, isn't it? I intend for my girls to receive the same education as my son. Have you read the latest paper by Doctor Armitage? It's quite fascinating."

Ava blinked, missing a beat. "I have indeed. It's pleasant to meet a gentleman who doesn't find it shocking, truly."

"I can imagine. Do your parents support your studies?"

She nodded, feeling more at ease now. Lord Thame read *Doctor Armitage*, which was an excellent start and a pleasant surprise.

"They do. However, I think they worry that my reputation as a... well, as a bluestocking, I suppose, will ruin my chances at marriage. I am, after all, not even engaged at the ancient age of twenty-six. It's rather ridiculous, don't you think? I am not searching for a suitor, and if I were, I wouldn't look for one in the *marriage mart*. I do not view myself as a mere animal looking to be possessed. It's quite repulsive, at times."

Lord Thame's expression was neutral, and he swirled his punch around his cup, saying nothing.

Ava cursed herself for a fool. It was all well and good to have those opinions – deep down, most people hated the marriage mart and the Season – but one didn't go around *airing* those thoughts. They certainly didn't air out their opinions to handsome, eligible men who had shown interest in them and read Doctor Armitage's papers.

You, Ava Devane, are a fool of the highest order, she told herself, *and it's no surprise you will be a spinster forever.*

She opened her mouth to try for an apology but closed it again at the horrified expression on Lord Thame's face.

But then, he wasn't looking at her. He was looking over her shoulder, at a remarkably beautiful woman in a sapphire blue silk gown swaying across the floor towards them, a slow smile spreading across her face.

Chapter Four

Dominic's head was reeling. It was far too early to say, of course, but really, Lady Ava seemed *perfect*. He'd seen how tenderly and lovingly she cared for her younger sister, and how her sister adored her in turn. She was obviously part of a loving family and spoke highly of her siblings and parents. She was interested in his children, in a way that was neither too fawning and false, nor too coolly polite.

She was intelligent, a woman who *studied*, and clearly an advocate for women's education. Dominic had always intended for his girls to go to university, if such a thing was possible, and to do so he would need a strong woman at his side to make it happen.

That had once been Marianne, and it was shockingly hard to find women who endorsed the education of other women.

And then she had told him that she hated the prospect of marriage and had no intention of marrying, and Dominic's heart plummeted.

Well, that was not ideal.

Don't give up so quickly, he scolded himself. *No sensible person could care for the marriage mart nonsense.*

He shifted, clearing his throat and taking another sip of his punch. Lady Ava had gone quiet, and an unusual moment of awkward silence had sprung up between them. Keen not to lose his advantage, Dominic was thinking of how to revive the conversation when his glance happened to slide upwards, over Lady Ava's shoulder, and he froze.

Ursula was making a beeline for them, eyes intent, her silk gown rustling about her. Dominic's heart dropped. There was no point in pretending he hadn't seen her – not that it would do any good, of course – and neither could he warn Lady Ava in any way.

Then Ursula was on them.

"Lord Thame, I wondered where you had gone!" she cooed. "Were we not dancing together for this last set?"

Dominic wholeheartedly cursed the woman. Lady Ava flinched, glancing up at him, wide-eyed. Ladies could not refuse a gentleman who asked them to dance, but a gentleman who double-booked his dance sets was a scandal in itself.

"No, Mrs Winslow, we were not." he said firmly, meeting Ava's eye. Her expression had shuttered itself, turning blank and neutral. "I beg your pardon if there was any confusion."

Ursula pouted, shuffling a little closer to him. "Well, we can always remedy that. I believe a new set is starting very shortly."

"Mrs Winslow, have you met Lady Ava Devane?" Dominic said desperately, gesturing towards Ava with his half-empty punch glass.

The women's gazes met, and Ursula all but scowled.

"Yes, in fact we have met, haven't we, Lady Ava? I believe we came Out during the same Seasons, did we not? I was nineteen, and Lady Ava was eighteen. What a fine time it was, was it not? Of course, I have since been married and widowed, whereas my poor friend had never had the fortune of being married, not even once. I always thought that was such a pity. Not even a betrothed, Ava? You poor dear. Still, I suppose we can't have all the luck, can we? I daresay you're quite happy at home, taking care of your parents and reading your books."

Lady Ava flinched. One didn't have to be well-versed in the language of Society Belles to hear the insults in what Ursula said.

Before Dominic could say or do anything – not that he had the slightest idea of what he might say – Ursula was at Ava's side, sliding her arm through Ava's elbow.

"My dear friend is very clever." Ursula said confidentially to Dominic, in much the same tone as she might have said that her friend had the pox. "Rather too clever for most gentlemen. I always joked that Ava was too covered in book dust, and that the gentlemen couldn't come near her without coughing and choking. Did I not, Ava? It was tremendously funny. But I daresay you don't mind, do you, Ava? You've always preferred dry old books and Latin to real people, haven't you? Some people are just like that, I suppose. They'd rather read about real life in books, rather than experiencing it for themselves. Now, you and I, Lord Thame, are people who like to *live* our lives. Don't you think?"

Ava had gone white, lips pressed together. Dominic opened his mouth, desperately racking his brain for something he could say to make Ursula stop, anything at all.

Ava gently slid her arm away from Ursula, her smile barely wavering.

"Well, I think *you* have lived enough life for all of us combined. Haven't you, Mrs Winslow? And what a varied life it has been for you. You have my congratulations."

There was something in what she said that made Ursula blink and narrow her eyes.

"Very varied, my dear. Now, you really mustn't keep Lord Thame all to yourself, you know. It's bad manners, and he's far too kind to say anything."

Ava pursed her lips. "You're right, of course. Do excuse me. Good evening, Lord Thame. Thank you for the dance."

And then, before he could say another word, Ava made a quick curtsey, first to him and then to Ursula. Ursula barely bobbed in return, and Ava strode off into the crowd, not once looking back.

Dominic swallowed hard, trying to tamp down his anger and frustration. He glanced down at Ursula, who was practically preening with triumph.

"It was so kind of you to dance with her." Ursula said confidentially. "Dear Lady Ava. She so rarely dances with anyone. I'm surprised to see her here this year, to be frank. The poor woman has done Season after Season, and not a sniff of a match. Do be careful she doesn't mistake your kindness for something else."

She leaned forward a little, as if about to follow up with something else, but Dominic had had enough. More than enough, really.

"I see." He said coolly, setting aside his half-empty punch cup with a *clack*. "Now, you wanted to dance, Mrs Winslow?"

Her face lit up. "Indeed, I did, Lord Thame."

"Well, I'm afraid I am not dancing at all for the rest of the night – I am quite fatigued. If you wish to find a partner for the next set, I suggest you hurry. Good evening, Mrs Winslow."

He didn't wait for a reply. Dominic made a quick, abrupt bow, and turned on his heel, marching away into the crowd. He could feel Ursula's gaze sizzling into his back, but pointedly did not allow himself to turn around.

He was in desperate pursuit of Ava. Pray, where on earth had she absconded?

I'll never find her in this crowd, Dominic thought, despairingly.

Dominic was ready to give up by the time he finally spotted them. It was Miss Trent that saved him, her vibrant red hair standing out in the crowd. He saw Ava immediately, deep in conversation with an older couple that he guessed were her parents. There was a woman who looked like an older version of Ava and had her hand resting on her belly, who was most likely Lady Connors. A gentleman and a lady who both had greying red hair seemed to be Miss Trent's parents, and he spotted Lady Suzanne, too.

He hesitated a little as he approached, wondering if he were about to interrupt a private conversation. Miss Trent saved him once again, spotting him at once and welcoming him into the group with a wide, good-natured smile.

"Lord Thame, how good to see you again! Ava and you danced remarkably well. Didn't they, Mama?"

Dominic stepped forward into the knot of people, aware that several assessing gazes were immediately levelled his way.

"She is a particularly graceful dancer." Dominic said smoothly, flashing Ava a quick smile. "It was my pleasure."

Ava returned his gaze steadily. With her olive skin, it was nearly impossible to tell if she were blushing or not at the compliment. He didn't think Ava was the sort of woman who tended to blush, in any case.

Introductions were made, and in no time, he was introduced to Lady Connors, Lord and Lady Mortensen, and Lord and Lady Trent, Miss Trent's parents.

"I'm afraid we're just leaving." Ava said, when the pleasantries were over. "Beverley is feeling a little unwell, so we thought it best to go home early. Of course, we don't want to cut Suzi's first ball short, but Lady Trent has kindly offered to chaperone her, and take her home afterwards."

"Ah, I see." Dominic said, flashing what he hoped was a sympathetic smile towards Lady Connors and trying to swallow his disappointment. What exactly had he hoped to achieve from this conversation, anyway? Another dance?

I couldn't dance with her again, not after I told Mrs Winslow I wasn't dancing, he thought. *I suppose I just... well, I just wanted her to know that I hadn't abandoned her in favour of Mrs Winslow.*

Ava was watching him narrowly, her expression unreadable

but undeniably pleasant. Lady Mortensen's gaze was flickering between them. Dominic had dealt with enough ambitious mammas to know what was going on. Lady Mortensen would know a great deal about him – any good mamma made it her business to know all the single men around. She would know roughly how much money he had, of his past, of his family, of any scandals attached to him, how eligible he was. She would be calculating all of this and measuring it against the interest he had shown to her daughter. Her gaze flicked once to Lady Suzanne, who was inspecting her dance card and showing Dominic no attention at all, and she seemed to give up on that idea.

"You really must visit us sometime, Lord Thame." Lady Mortensen said smoothly, as he'd known she would. "Please, don't stand on ceremony. Leave your card as soon as you can, and just drop in at any time. We love visitors."

By that she means we love single, eligible gentlemen visitors, Dominic thought wryly. Aloud, he thanked her, and made a bow.

It was a pity that Ava was going home. No doubt she could have stayed on with Lady Trent, but clearly that was not going to happen.

They all bid their goodbyes, and Dominic found himself watching Ava disappear across the ballroom, with her mother linking her arm on one side and her older sister on the other. Miss Trent and Lady Suzanne disappeared for the next dance, and he hastily made his excuses before Lord and Lady Trent could badger him into joining a card game.

***

"There you are." Dominic muttered, gripping Richard's shoulder and manoeuvring him towards the balcony. "I want to talk to you."

Richard, who seemed to have been entertaining himself by standing in a corner and watching other people talk and dance, showed no objection to been pushed out of the hot ballroom.

"I see that Lady Ava Devane has gone home." Richard observed in a low voice. "Are you disappointed?"

"Wait until we get outside, you wretch."

The two men crossed the balcony, which was currently full

of young ladies and men, fanning themselves and resting before the dancing resumed. It was past midnight, but the ball would continue for hours. The final revellers would totter out towards their carriage just prior to daybreak, having waltzed ceaselessly through the night. They would travel home as the sun rose and would then sleep until noon.

Dominic felt tired just imagining it. Parenthood certainly sapped a person's energy.

The terrace was quiet. No doubt the darkness put off most of the visitors, along with the steep and forbidden stairs. Once again, Richard and Dominic leaned against the stone wall, and stood in silence for a moment or two.

"She intrigues you, doesn't she?" Richard said, after a moment. "Lady Ava."

Dominic pursed his lips. "Yes," he admitted. "She does. What do you think of her?"

"She strikes me as an intelligent woman with a mind of her own. Very pretty, too. Although of course that is not what you are looking for."

"No, it is not. I introduced myself to her family, at least. That... that feels like a start. But she is not interested in marriage."

Richard eyed him. "Not interested at all? She seemed interested in you, if only because you're an intelligent man who isn't flirting too hard with her."

Dominic raked a hand through his hair, and sighed. "I don't know, I don't *know*. I enjoyed her conversation, and I flattered myself that she enjoyed my company."

"I'd say so. From what I saw, she has no scruples abandoning someone who bores her. Do you think the children would like her? Do you think she would like them?"

"She loves her family." Dominic said slowly. "She's fond of children – at least, that's what she said – and her younger sister clearly adores her. There were times when I thought that she... no, I'd better not think about that. The thing is, I am looking for a marriage of convenience. A partnership, if you will. I need to be clear about that from the beginning. I don't expect love, not like I had with Marianne, and part of me thinks that Lady Ava will appreciate that sort of arrangement."

"And what does the rest of you think about it? The part that isn't focused solely on logic and your children."

Dominic flinched, not sure whether that was meant to be an insult or not. He glanced over at his friend, only to find that Richard's face was shadowed, his expression unreadable.

"You are a fine judge of character." He said softly. "What do you think of Lady Ava?"

Richard was quiet for a moment or two. "I think she's a fine woman. Better than Mrs Winslow, at the very least. But you need to tread carefully. A marriage of convenience is all very well, but her parents are clearly not interested in forcing her into a loveless marriage. If they suspect your intentions are not romantic, not *honourable...*"

"My intentions are honourable!"

"Some parents might disagree. You're a good man and you will make her happy, but as you say, your proposal is more of a partnership than a marriage. Lady Ava and you might never have your own children, might never be more than friends. Some parents might not want that for their daughter."

Dominic was quiet, absorbing this. "But I cannot possibly trick Lady Ava into a marriage. I can't. I wouldn't."

"Of course not, you fool. You must tell *her* the whole truth, but her parents might want to see the semblance of romance. Lady Ava strikes me as a woman who thinks for herself, which is quite well and good, but it doesn't do to be too open about these arrangements. Do you see?"

He did see. Dominic leaned back against the wall, feeling the sharp, rough edges of stone dig into his back through his clothes. Inside, another dance had started, and most of the chattering youngsters on the balcony had hurried back inside. He could hear strains of music drifting out of the open doors, down to where Richard and he stood, forgotten and unnoticed.

He knew this was how Richard liked to live – standing apart, able to see and observe others when they were unaware of him – but Dominic felt... well, he felt as if part of him was missing.

If Marianne were alive, they would have been inside, dancing, drinking, laughing. Even if they had come outside, they would have leaned on the stone parapet and talked, comfortable in each other's company and utterly content.

But now it felt as though life were passing him by, washing

over him like the music played by unseen musicians, fading away and a little muffled. Dominic considered reaching for his pipe but thought better of it. Marianne had always hated that habit.

"Lady Mortensen invited me to call on them sometime." He heard himself say. "I will take her up on her invitation and see where it goes from there. Now, Richard, do you want to stay and watch people dance for another few hours, or shall we leave?"

Richard gave a wry smile. "I think you know that I've wanted to leave since I arrived."

"Then why *did* you arrive at all?"

"Not at all your business, is it?" Richard retorted easily. "Come on, let's go to an inn and have a drink, shall we?"

Chapter Five

The carriage door was barely closed on them before the others burst out into questions.

"Why was Lord Thame talking to you, Ava?"

"How strange of him to approach us in that way."

"What aren't you telling us?"

"Did you dance a *waltz*, Ava?"

The last comment was from Beverley, who seemed somewhat peeved. She did not approve of waltzing, although she had given into the fashions of Society and allowed waltzing at her balls, between respectably married couples or engaged couples. Or, at the very least, between a couple who had an *understanding*. Not, of course, that Beverley was hosting any social events now that she was so close to her confinement. Suzi was not here, of course, and Gordon was travelling back alone to his lodgings. That meant that the carriage was a little more comfortable with the four of them, instead of six.

Ava held up her hands to ward off questions, laughing.

"Mama, Papa, *please*. One at a time, won't you?"

Lady Mortensen pursed her lips. "Come, Ava, it was very singular of him, coming up to speak to us all like that."

"Yes, how very strange for a gentleman to speak to people at a *ball*." Ava remarked under her breath, smoothing out her skirts.

It didn't matter that she felt a little shaky, and the memory of Lord Thame's smile kept replaying itself over and over in her mind. Her father was sitting opposite her in the carriage, holding his newspaper to the light of window to read by. He met her eye over the rim of the paper, wiggled his eyebrows, and flashed a sympathetic grin.

Ava rolled her eyes and suppressed a fond smile. There'd be no help from *that* quarter, then.

On cue, Lady Mortensen leaned forward. "*Did* you waltz with him, Ava? I didn't see Lord Thame's name on your dance card."

Ava tugged the offending item off her wrist. She hated wearing the dance cards on her wrist. People always eyed the dance cards of single women, to see how popular they were – or how popular they were *not*. Ava had a few paltry names on her card, in stark contrast to Suzi's, which was almost full.

"He came up and asked me to dance just before the set started." She responded coolly. "I daresay he was bored."

Beverley pursed her lips at that. "You don't give yourself enough credit, Ava. If you would only *apply* yourself, I'm sure you could attract more gentlemen than you do. It is not so difficult to be *fascinating,* not for a woman of your intellect."

Ava sighed, leaning back against the soft, newly upholstered cushions of the carriage, and stared out of the window.

Silvery moonlight streamed down from a clear sky, illuminating the landscape as they rushed by. She'd never had a talent for painting – which was an *appropriate* talent for a young lady and could be referred to as an *accomplishment* – but at times like this, Ava wished that she could.

I wonder if Lord Thame is observing the night sky, too. Oh, stop it, you foolish woman!

The art of being *fascinating* was one that Ava had never quite grasped. It involved more than simply being tremendously interested in whatever a gentleman had to say – although of course that was part of it. It was easy enough for a man to find a listening ear in a woman. Debutantes feared being marked as 'chatter-boxes', and were careful to keep their few words smooth and carefully set into the conversation so as not to dominate.

A fascinating woman had a way of telling a story that thrilled her listeners. Her stories were of course brief, never obscure, and always concerning a subject that her listener – always a gentleman – would enjoy. Her stories and conversation must draw in a person, and make him want to converse more with her, make him feel as if speaking to her was *easy*. However, she must not leave him feeling as if she were simply good-natured, and that *everyone* found it easy to speak to her.

A fascinating woman made a man feel special. It was an art. A skill, Beverley had said.

For her part, Ava had never seen the importance of making a man feel special. In her experience, men seeking out *fascinating* women were simply *not* special.

Besides, Beverley was a big hypocrite. She certainly hadn't fascinated *her* husband – Lord Connors adored his wife, and she had not been interested in him for at least half a Season, despite his awkward efforts to entrance her.

That didn't matter though. Ava reminded herself, as she tried to keep herself awake in the gently rocking carriage, that Beverley was married and had a child on the way, and so was above reproach.

"Ava?" Beverley continued waspishly. "Are you *listening* to me?"

"Of course I am listening, my darling sister."

Beverley snorted, and Lady Mortensen leaned forward again, tapping Ava's knee.

"Tell me everything. I want to hear the whole interaction between Lord Thame and you."

Ava sighed. She would get no rest until the story was told. Beverley was staying with them overnight at Devane House, and they would both simply follow Ava to her rooms, bombarding her with questions, and Ava did so dearly want to sleep.

"Lord Larchmere and he approached me while I was talking to Gordon, Suzi, and Willi."

"Oh, him." Beverley said tartly. She was not fond of Lord Larchmere. "I cannot stand that man. He's so prissy and looks at one as if one has said something remarkably stupid."

"In your case, my dear Beverley, that is probably true."

Beverley delivered a forceful strike to her sister's shin.

"Stop it, both of you!" Lady Mortensen scolded. "You are not children."

Ava stuck out her tongue at her older sister and received an elbow in her ribs for her troubles.

"Well, as I was saying, Lord Larchmere introduced us, then Lord Thame asked me to dance. So, we danced. Afterwards, we retreated to the refreshment tables, and had punch. That's all."

She had, of course, omitted their earlier meeting on the terrace. Ava knew she would be scolded for going down to the dark terrace alone.

"How did it end?" Lady Mortensen persisted. "How did the conversation end? You were not talking to him when I found you."

Ava bit her lip, glancing back out of the carriage window. "Mrs Winslow joined us and made unpleasant remarks about my monopolising Lord Thame. I took my leave."

Lady Mortensen clucked her tongue. "Oh, *her*. Do you

conjecture that she is endeavouring to court his affections?"

"I think so," Beverley interjected. "Everyone knows she's looking for a new husband, and Lord Thame is a handsome man."

Ava picked at her skirts. "Indeed, she may lay claim to him. I am no simpleton to engage in a rivalry with Mrs. Winslow."

Ava's mother eyed her for a long moment. "Ava, don't be obtuse," she said, after a moment. "You are too clever to act silly. You must know what we are thinking."

"Yes," Ava sighed. "You are thinking that Lord Thame has an interest in me. I can assure you he does not."

"And why not?" Beverley burst out. "What exactly is wrong with *you*? You are a suitable age for him, you are pretty, you are clever, you are interesting. Why should Lord Thame turn up his nose at you?"

Ava swallowed past a lump in her throat. Her family's praise should have made her feel good about herself, but unfortunately, it had the opposite effect.

"I am six-and-twenty, Beverley. According to Society's norms, I am no longer in the bloom of youth. I daresay Lord Thame wants a sprightly young debutante, or perhaps someone as elegant and wealthy as Mrs Winslow."

Beverley and Lady Mortensen glanced at each other.

"I won't have this sort of self-defeating talk, Ava." Lady Mortensen said firmly. "Only a simpleton would choose *Mrs Winslow* over *you*."

Ava smiled sadly at her mother. "I know that you believe that. But, as I said, I doubt he will stay interested for very long. If he *is* interested. I think we have seen the last of Lord Thame, take heed of my words."

The ground beneath the carriage wheels changed from smooth cobbles to well-raked gravel, and Ava knew that they were nearly home. The gravel made up a long, winding drive, which led up to Devane House, their London home.

It was a pretty building, smaller than their country home, but neat and cosy. There were gardens around the house, again smaller than their country gardens, but pretty and impressive for London. Ava could see that almost all of the lights were off in the windows. The household would be asleep, except for the few servants who had stayed up to get their employers to bed. She realized with a start that it was well past midnight, probably inching towards one in the morning.

The carriage drew to a halt in front of the house, and Beverley moved to get out first. She moved slowly and carefully, her hand resting protectively on her belly, and Lady Mortensen and the footmen fussed over her, breathing a sigh of relief when her slippers rested on solid ground once again.

Ava moved to climb out next but was halted by her father taking her hand.

"Whether this Lord Thame is interested or not," he said, quietly so that the others could not hear, "you are a remarkable woman, my clever girl. If he does not see that, he's not worthy of you. I would rather see you single for the rest of your life than married to a man who does not value you."

Ava blinked, taken aback. She swallowed hard, tears pricking at her eyes, and opened her mouth to reply.

""Ava! Depart, you impish rascal! Have you succumbed to slumber within?" Beverley called, and Ava blinked, coming back to herself.

Lord Mortensen smiled sadly and reached out to touch her cheek.

"Go on, then." He said, and there was nothing left for Ava to do but climb out into the cold night.

She was bone tired, and her feet kept twitching as if longing to waltz once again.

***

"Well, I am glad you had a fine time, milady." Lizzie announced, carefully laying Ava's modest jewels in a velvet-lined box.

Lizzie, Ava's maid, was remarkably efficient. The fire in Ava's room was laid, and her night-things were hanging in front of the fire to warm them. Her bedclothes were turned back, ready for her to fall into bed and go right to sleep.

Ava stood before her mirror, yawning, and let her maid neatly unbutton and unlace her from the layers and layers of clothing, stripping away the stiff garments and the expensive silks and lace, folding them away with a practised hand.

"I'm sorry you had to stay up so late." Ava said, smothering another yawn. "If these clothes were easier to get out of, I'd undress myself."

"I don't mind, milady." Lizzie responded, turning her attention to Ava's hair. "Indeed, I am confident I shall indulge in a leisurely repose tomorrow."

Ava shook her head, letting her hair tumble down from where it had been thickly pinned in place. Her head tingled, and she couldn't suppress a sigh of relief.

"This," Ava announced, "is the best part of any ball. Getting out of the wretched corsets and itchy fabrics and taking all of the endless hairpins out of my hair. I can feel *human* again."

Lizzie chuckled. "I can't say that I envy you, wearing all this. Tell me, though, did you dance with a fine gentleman tonight? Lady Connors was talking to her maid about it, very loudly."

"Lord Thame." Ava responded, shuffling her way into her loose nightgown. "He asked me to dance, and my family are acting as if it were a proposal."

"I thought such things usually preceded a proposal."

She shrugged. "They can, but gentlemen are *obliged* to do certain things. The rules aren't as strict for them as they are for ladies, but ladies aren't permitted to show interest in gentlemen. The gentlemen must make all the moves, so something as simple as a dance can be seen as *interest*."

Lizzie sighed, lacing up the back of Ava's nightgown. "It sounds dreadfully complicated, milady."

"Oh, it is. And they haven't even considered the possibility that he asked me to dance as a joke, or as part of a wager."

Lizzie's nimble fingers paused. "A joke? A wager? What do you mean, milady?"

Ava rolled her shoulders, avoiding her maid's gaze in the mirror. She felt a little embarrassed, and wished she hadn't said anything.

"I'm a notable spinster, now." she muttered. "I've turned down a great many gentlemen, and I'm known for being... well, rather forbidding. There are some gentlemen who take such a thing as a challenge. They don't wish to marry me, of course – I'm too old for most of them – but gentlemen who highly value their powers of seduction rather enjoy making firm old spinsters fall in love with them. To prove a point, you see. To make a conquest. I've seen it happen before. A few notable flirts have tried it with me, too. Fortunately, they were insufferable, or I would have ended up looking very silly."

Lizzie pressed her lips together in a thin line.

"That is awful, milady. Truly awful. Are there really men who find such a thing funny? Oh, it's so cruel. If they are found out, they ought to be *made* to marry you."

Ava winced. "What, and the poor spinster finds herself married to a man who despises her? No, thank you. That feels like more of a punishment, and a great deal of humiliation."

Lizzie snorted to herself, obviously not convinced. Ava watched her maid bustle around the room, putting things away, restoring order.

Lizzie was roughly the same age as Ava herself, and they had been together since they were both children. Ava would not like to have any other maid, and considered Lizzie a friend just like Willi, or even Suzi. Lizzie was round-faced and very sweet, with flaxen-blonde hair tucked away under an old-fashioned cap with a ruffle around it. She had a temper, though, and was clearly already seething at the idea of some rakish gentlemen playing a trick on some unsuspecting spinster.

"And do you think Lord Thame is playing a joke on you, milady?" Lizzie asked after a moment or two. The thought had clearly been weighing on her.

"I don't know." Ava sighed, climbing into bed. The sheets were warm – a warming pan had been freshly removed from between them – and she settled in with a contented sigh. "He seemed too kind for that. He's a widower with children, and usually the gentlemen who play such tricks are young, single simpletons."

Lizzie pursed her lips, absently smoothing down the quilt over the top of Ava's bed. The fire was starting to die down, a flicker at the end of the room. The chill was already creeping back into the room, but Ava was now safely wrapped up in her bedclothes and did not care.

"Would you like him to be paying serious court to you, then?" Lizzie asked.

Ava flinched. Few – if any – maids would be so bold as to ask that question, but the relationship between Lizzie and her was different. She felt obliged to answer the question.

"I don't know." Ava responded honestly. "I... I liked him, but I don't wish to be disappointed or hurt. I've been single for so long, and it's comfortable."

Lizzie nodded slowly, as if the answer was what she'd expected.

"Sleep well, milady. Do you need anything else?"

"No, thank you."

Lizzie disappeared, taking the candle with her, and Ava rested her head on the pillow and closed her eyes. She would dream of waltzing tonight, she just knew it.

Chapter Six

It was after midnight by the time Dominic's carriage trundled up to the wrought-iron gates of Pemberton House.

He'd never bothered renaming the house. Their townhouse was bought in haste, after Marianne's death, large enough to keep the children and the household, while allowing Dominic to be close to his work and his friends.

They'd moved out to the country after Daniella was born. It had seemed a good idea, raising their children in the peace and quiet of the countryside.

But then Marianne had died, and Dominic had found that his friends were few, his family non-existent, and he missed London more than he would ever have thought possible.

Footmen hurried out to open the gates, and the carriage rolled through.

The house was almost pitch black, with just a few lights on in a few select windows. Dominic could see his own bedroom window from here, a fine room on the second floor with a balcony. He fancied he could see his valet's silhouette moving to and fro behind the curtains, getting things ready for his master's return.

The butler, Peeves, was waiting on the doorstep, hands folded in a dignified manner, waiting for Dominic to extricate himself from the carriage.

"I trust you had an enjoyable evening, sir?" he asked politely, and Dominic flashed a tired smile.

"Enjoyable enough, Peeves, thank you. Please, get yourself to bed – I feel terribly guilty over you waiting up for me."

Peeves gave a benevolent smile and said nothing.

"The children are in bed, I take it?" Dominic asked, shrugging his way out of his coat. He hated the fitted style of the new fashions, which were so tightly shaped to a gentleman's shoulders and back that he couldn't shrug his way in and out of his own coat. Peeves was obliged to help. Free of his constricting coat, Dominic rolled his shoulders with a sigh.

"They are, sir."

"Were there any... incidents?" Dominic finished lamely.

Peeves' eyes flickered. "I believe there was a small incident, sir. Perhaps you should speak to Nurse Emily. She is not asleep."

Dominic pressed his lips together. "I see. Thank you, Peeves. And get yourself to bed. I mean it."

He climbed the stairs, the thick carpet muffling his footsteps. The house was eerily quiet, and he knew that regardless of what had happened earlier in the evening, the children were asleep now.

The second floor was divided into two wings – one for himself and various spare bedrooms, and the other for the children.

They slept in the nursery, of course, although Daniella was starting to ask for her own room. There was a series of rooms for Emily – bedroom, sitting room, washroom, and so on – and another series of rooms for the governess, whenever one was to be engaged.

Daniella was eight, and soon she would need her own tutor for things Emily could not teach her.

A large, white-painted door with various child's pictures pasted to the front of it was the nursery, and no light came from underneath the door. Emily's room, however, which was next door, had a thin bar of light coming from underneath.

He knocked softly on the door, and it creaked open.

"You're back, sir." Emily said, smiling tiredly. "I hope you had a good time."

She was somewhere in her forties, with a lined face and iron-grey hair scooped back into a knot at the base of her neck. She had been a maid in the house when Dominic was small and had assisted his nurse at times. When he grew up and got married, he had enlisted Emily to come with him, and had subsequently brought her back to London with him. She was a kind and softly spoken woman, who nevertheless had the knack of making children mind her. Steven adored her, as did baby Maria, and even Daniella, to an extent.

However, Daniella was more difficult to manage lately, and that was shown in the lines of strain around Emily's eyes.

"It was a pleasant evening." he responded. "Can I kiss the children goodnight, or will I wake them?"

"They're sleeping soundly. If you're quiet, sir. And... sir, I would like to talk, if you have a moment."

He swallowed hard. "About Daniella."

She nodded wordlessly, and the knot of tension in his chest tightened.

He slipped next door, easing open the nursery door.

The nursery was a large, square room, with one half entirely dominated by toys, a blackboard, and three desks and chairs arranged around the blackboard. The alphabet was carefully written on the board, no doubt for the benefit of the two youngest.

The other half of the nursery was much neater, with wardrobes and little trunks set out, and three narrow beds set side by side near the window. Steven was afraid of the dark, but Nurse Emily had a great fear of fire, and would not allow him to have a candle. As a compromise, the curtains were flung wide, allowing silvery moonlight to creep into the room.

It seemed to reassure Steven, although it meant that the children woke with the rising sun most mornings.

An elongated slash of light from the hallway spilled into the nursery, enough to illuminate Dominic's way as he tiptoed across the room.

He went to Maria's bed first, still a baby's cot with high sides to prevent her rolling out. She was tangled up in her bedsheets, her baby-thin hair sticking to her forehead.

"Goodnight, Maria." Dominic whispered, pressing a kiss to her head. Out of them all, he thought Maria would grow up to look the most like her mother. She already had Marianne's soft brown hair and large, thoughtful brown eyes.

He moved to the next bed, where Steven slept huddled under a pile of blankets, only a shock of brown hair sticking above the sheets. Steven was too young to remember much about his mother and had adjusted to having only one parent well enough. Dominic pressed a kiss to the top of his head, smoothing the shock of tangled hair as best he could.

"Goodnight, Steven."

He moved to the bed of his oldest child next.

Daniella was all Dominic's child. She had his fair hair and slanted, inquisitive eyes, and his tendency to withdraw herself and become aloof when the situation was not to her liking. Even in her sleep, her brow was furrowed, making her look older than her not-

44

quite-eight years, and she curled up tightly on her side.

"Goodnight, Daniella." Dominic murmured, leaning down to kiss her cheek. He was pulling back, intending to creep out as quietly as he'd come, when Daniella's eyes fluttered open, heavy with sleep.

"Papa?"

He winced. The last thing any of them wanted was for the children to wake up and decide they had had enough of sleeping.

"Go to sleep, Dannie. It is very late."

Daniella rubbed her eye with a fist. "I wanted to stay up and see you before I went to bed."

"I'm sure you did, darling, but it's too late for you. You need your sleep, remember? I said goodnight after dinner, didn't I?"

She scowled. "It's not the same."

"It won't happen often, dearest. Now close your eyes and go back to sleep again. It will be morning in just a moment."

He turned to go, but Daniella spoke again.

"Papa, will you tell Emily I'm sorry, please? I was very unkind."

He turned, frowning, but Daniella was already falling back asleep, her lashes fluttering on her cheeks and her face finally softening.

He sighed and shook his head, tiptoeing back to the door. He took one last look at his children, all quietly sleeping, safe in their nursery, and a lump rose to his throat.

I'm doing my best, Marianne. Please, believe me. I'm doing my best.

Swallowing hard, Dominic shut the door softly.

He slipped into Emily's sitting room, where the fire was banked and two armchairs were angled towards the hearth. He sniffed, smelling a delicious and familiar scent.

"Is that cocoa, Emily?"

She smiled at him over her shoulder, setting out two steaming mugs. "Indeed it is, sir. It's late, and you'll need a little something to help you sleep."

"Thank you, Emily, that's kind. I did my best not to disturb the children, but Daniella awoke. She said... said I should tell you that she is sorry, that she was unkind."

Emily sighed, shaking her head. "Oh, the poor little love. She

45

was already forgiven, but I daresay it weighed heavy on her. She never apologised before she went to sleep, you see."

She sank down into one armchair and gestured for Dominic to take the other.

He obeyed, perching nervously on the edge of the seat. This was Emily's domain, *her* rooms, and he always reminded himself that they were not *his* rooms at the moment, not like the rest of the house.

"Can I ask what happened?"

Emily bit her lip, staring into the fire for a long moment.

"She wanted to stay up to greet you when you came home." Emily said at last. "Well, I knew you wouldn't be back before midnight, if not later, and you know how grouchy she gets if she doesn't sleep. I said no, of course. But that wasn't the end of it, not this time. They often try to wrangle a later bedtime, but I know all the tricks, and I stay firm. But this time..." Emily hesitated, eyes flickering around.

Dominic swallowed hard. "This time, she threw a tantrum, didn't she?"

Emily nodded silently.

Daniella's tantrums had only appeared in the last few years. As the oldest child, she had known her mother very well, and adored her. She had taken the loss very hard, refusing to accept that Marianne was gone. Of course, it was a difficult concept for a child to grasp, and Dominic himself was struggling with the loss.

The tantrums had appeared shortly after their return to London. She would scream, cry, fling herself to the floor, and object to the simplest of requests which had never bothered her before.

"Tell me." Dominic said, gathering his courage.

"She requested to stay up until you returned, and of course I said she could not. She insisted, informing me that she is virtually the lady of the house and as such I must obey her."

Dominic felt colour rise to his cheeks.

"And then, when I refused to budge, she hurled a small china kitten at me." Emily added, matter-of-factly. "It did not hit me but smashed against the wall. I believe it was a present from her grandfather. The shards have all been swept up. I'm afraid it couldn't be saved."

46

Dominic swallowed hard, feeling equal parts shame and fury.

"I... I am sorry, Emily, I am so sorry. I do not condone her behaviour, not in the slightest. You were right to exercise your authority in that way, and she will be punished for this tomorrow. Severely."

Emily waved a hand. "She was punished last night. This was shortly after six o' clock, at least two hours before she would have retired. I scolded her, made her clean up the smashed kitten – with my supervision, of course – and sent her straight to bed. She seemed a little shocked at herself, I must say."

"And so she should." Dominic raked a hand through his hair. "I cannot allow her to behave like that. Emily, I cannot apologise enough. Please, *please* don't leave us."

Emily chuckled, taking a sip of her cocoa. "Don't fret, sir. I shan't leave. Children do throw tantrums, at times. They behave badly and act selfishly because they are still learning, and they don't know otherwise. Especially children of Daniella's age. Only a few years ago, she was a small child, and had just about everything her own way. The world was easy, and constantly made way for her. Now she is growing up, and she is learning that things are expected of her, and she cannot always have her own way. Children misbehave, sir. It's quite ordinary. However, these fault do need to be corrected, and soon. A small child who throws tantrums is easily managed, but a grown woman or even a girl..." she trailed off meaningfully. "This must be dealt with, sir. And soon."

Dominic swallowed hard, still feeling mortified. The truth was that a nurse couldn't hold authority over a girl like Daniella for very long. Soon Daniella would start to understand her place in the world, and she would realize that her family paid Emily's wages. Besides, Emily's job was never meant to involve wrangling a difficult growing girl.

"She needs a mother, doesn't she?" Dominic murmured. "I try my best, Emily, believe me, but between managing the estate and searching for a new wife, I feel as though I am never here."

"Your children love you, sir." Emily soothed. "And for what it's worth, they mind you, when you are here. But I do need help to correct Daniella's behaviour. Steven is a sweet boy, but he is growing too, and Maria already has a great deal of spirit."

Dominic nodded, eyeing his cocoa and thinking hard. Few people knew about his search for a wife, but Emily was one of them. She deserved to know, and he trusted her entirely. Besides, she would need to work alongside whatever woman he married too, so it was fair that she be warned.

"I encountered a lady this evening who appears to meet the requisites." He said, his voice loud in the quiet room. "She seems... intriguing."

"How lovely, sir. Are you fond of her?"

He raked a hand through his hair again. "Fond? Well, I suppose I am, at that. I hardly know her, of course. She is intelligent, and an advocate for women's education. She is of a reasonable age – I said before that I didn't want any debutantes or silly girls raising my children – and she is much loved by her family. She likes children, too. But she also mentioned a disinclination to marry. She is twenty-six and not married, so perhaps she would turn down my offer."

Emily pursed her lips, thinking. "She sounds like a fine woman. Is she pretty?"

Dominic bit his lip, conjuring up a picture of Ava and her smooth olive skin, laughing hazel eyes, and her thick mane of dark hair piled up on her head.

"Very pretty." He managed at last. "At least, I thought so."

"Well, sir, of course I don't presume to advise you in this, but why not tell her the whole truth?"

He nodded slowly. "I think that's the best thing for me to do, Emily."

***

Dominic made his way along to his room, the cocoa sitting warmly in his stomach and already making him feel sleepy.

His room was simple – Marianne and he had never liked showy décor – and his valet, Jasper, was humming to himself as he polished a mirror.

He glanced over at his master and flashed a quick smile.

"Good evening, my Lord. Pray, have you exhausted all your capacities for dancing?"

Dominic chuckled, tugging at his cravat. Jasper materialized in front of him, gently but firmly pushing his hands away and unpicking the knot himself.

"You might say that. Not that I danced a great deal, although I did manage to dance the scandalous waltz."

"And what's the verdict, my Lord? Is it as shocking as everyone claims?"

Dominic swallowed, remembering how Ava had felt in his arms.

Stop it, you fool. You're about to propose a marriage of convenience to the woman, not seduce her into falling in love.

"I would say so." He managed at last. "I am paying an important call tomorrow, by the way. Would you pick out a suitable outfit?"

Jasper, who loved fashion and whose opinion on Dominic's clothing was rarely asked, fought not to beam with joy.

"Of course, sir. I shall pick out a truly fantastic outfit for you."

"Wonderful." Dominic muttered, already regretting asking for help.

Chapter Seven

Ava woke at about ten o' clock, and yawned leisurely, stretching up her arms above her head. Her bed was soft and warm, and light streamed in through the cracked-open curtains.

There was no sign of Lizzie – she wouldn't wake Ava early on the mornings after a ball – but a ruffled yellow dress was set out for her, a nice simple one that would be easy to slip into herself.

Not that there would be much to do today, Ava reflected. They would all be recovering. After two o' clock, the calling hours could begin. Usually, nobody called on the Devanes after a ball, but this was Suzi's come-out, so likely there would be a few interested gentlemen calling on her. That was hours away, though.

Ava slipped out of bed, washing quickly and pulling on the yellow gown. It was one of the daring new fashions, where a gown fastened at the front instead of the back. It wasn't suitable to a social occasion, of course, or even to go walking in the Park, but it was perfectly fine to wear to a family meal, when lounging about one's own house.

In a few moments, she was skipping downstairs, leaving her hair loose to flop around her shoulders, still smothering a yawn.

She could hear the family in the dining room. Usually, breakfast was over and eaten by half past nine at the latest, but of course everyone was tired this morning. No doubt they had only just come down.

Ava paused in the hall, tying back her hair in a simple, childish plait, tying the end with a yellow ribbon. After all, it wouldn't do to have hair flopping in her food while she ate.

Then Ava heard her own name spoken and paused.

"Best not to tell her."

That was Lord Mortensen.

"Do you think she won't find out?" Beverley interjected, her voice thin and shrill, the way it got when she was anxious. "Ava's not a swooning miss. Besides, if she doesn't hear from us, she'll hear from somebody else."

"This isn't *fair*, it's so *unfair*!" Suzi wept.

It was the tears in Suzi's wobbly voice that made Ava push open the dining room door.

The whole family was there – excepting Gordon, who would probably still be in bed at his lodgings – and they all glanced up at once, guilt written on their features.

"Darling, you're awake." Lady Mortenson managed.

Ava swallowed hard. A feeling of dread coiled itself in her stomach.

"Pray, what is transpiring?"

They all glanced at each other, and she knew then that it would be much worse than she could have imagined. Something bad had happened. Something very bad.

Beverley moved first. For the first time, Ava noticed a selection of various newspapers and scandal sheets spread out over the table. That wasn't surprising, as the scandal sheets would always report heavily on the first ball of the Season. A pretty, enterprising young woman like Suzi would be sure to get a mention.

Wordlessly, Beverley pushed one of the scandal sheets towards her. Ava picked it up, heart thumping.

Had Suzi done something wrong? Had she made some mistake, something truly unforgivable?

Ava's mind reeled with all the nauseating possibilities. She imagined Suzi caught unchaperoned with a man – accidental, of course, but Society didn't care much whether it was accidental or deliberate – or snubbing her hostess, or offending someone powerful...

She drew in a deep breath and began to read. The scandal sheet was turned to the front page.

A Shocking Start To The Season!

As esteemed aficionados will ascertain, this periodical diligently strives to elucidate all the paramount truths pertaining to the Social Season, along with a plethora of clandestine revelations and scandalous morsels diligently veiled by others. Naturally, one always hopes for an intriguing start to the Season. The first Ball of the Season often sets the tone for the months to come, highlighting key players, characters to watch, and developments which we shall observe with great interest are set into motion.

This year, the start comes in the form of the Worthington's Ball – a very 'worthy' occasion and naturally attended by everybody. One expects some minor disasters – a clumsy debutante spilling a glass of punch down a gentleman's silk waistcoat, a nervy young lady missing out the steps to a dance and humiliating herself and her partner, or even a fine gown being trod upon, the hem coming away and the poor lady in question fleeing into the night in shame.

This year, the first Scandal of the Season was taken up by none other than Lady Ava Devane.

Ava stopped reading, sucking in a shaky breath. Scandal? What scandal? Was it her standing on the terrace? She shouldn't have done that, but it wasn't as if anyone else was there. She continued reading, not wanting to, but needing to all the same.

Lady Ava, as many will know, is an unremarkable spinster whose name has not often graced the pages of this magazine. After a marvellous start to her social career as a beautiful and intriguing young woman – if not fascinating or particularly accomplished – the years have ticked by for poor Lady Ava, and still no marriage.

Of course, this author sympathizes with Lady Ava – who would not? At the advanced age of twenty-six, with her youth ebbing away, the poor lady has had no engagements, no great romances, no tragic heartbreak, and no real prospects. As a confirmed spinster and a notable bluestocking, one might concede that Lady Ava herself is to blame for this sad state of affairs. Her acid tongue and unladylike interests have successfully repelled any suitable men, leaving her a rather comical figure this Season.

Imagine this author's surprise to see Lady Ava turning her attention to none other than Lord Dominic Broughton, the highly eligible Marquess of Thame. Lady Ava was observed spending a great deal of time with the unfortunate and good-natured Marquess, deep in conversation. She was reported to have entirely monopolized the Marquess, determinedly turning away young hopeful ladies of better standing than herself, and even coaxing the widower into the rather scandalous waltz.

It is, of course, entirely natural for Lady Ava to turn her attentions to finding a husband before it is too late, but this author must beg her not to make a fool of herself in this regard. Leave the handsome, eligible gentlemen to the debutantes, we beg her, and seek out a man more suitable to her age, station, and character.

To the Marquess, we say: beware! Somebody has her eye on you, and if you are not careful, you shall be thoroughly caught.

And to you, Lady Ava Devane, we say this, simply: for shame, Lady Ava! For shame!

***

Ava read the whole passage again, in case she'd somehow missed a crucial element.

It can't be real, she kept telling herself. *It must be an unpleasant misunderstanding. This isn't what happened at all.*

She glanced up, and found all of them staring at her, with mingled horror and sympathy.

"I... I didn't monopolise him." she managed, her voice sounding hoarse to her own ears. Suddenly her yellow gown, which had seemed so fresh and colourful upstairs, was garish and ugly. Her plaited hair was suddenly ridiculous, and she fought the urge to tear out the yellow ribbon and wind her hair into a more grown-up knot at the back of her head. "He asked *me* to dance. I only had a conversation with him. I only..."

"We are aware, my dearest." Lord Mortensen declared, swiftly seizing the paper from her delicate grasp. He crumpled it into a tight ball, his knuckles visibly straining as they turned a pallid shade. "You know how malicious these writers can get. No doubt it's written by some woman who fancied the Marquess herself, or some gentleman who tried to flirt with you."

53

Ava lowered herself upon the seat with great force, experiencing a distressing sensation in her constitution.

As the scandal sheet had rightly said, she had rarely graced their pages. Why would she? There'd been a few paragraphs on her coming-out – back when she was eighteen and considered just 'young enough' for a man of thirty, and nobody knew about her interests. She had been mentioned in passing, but never on her own merit, and it was never anything beyond a sentence or two.

And now, this. A full article, dripping with spite and glee, turning her into some ridiculous old harridan, pursuing a man.

That wasn't it at all.

"They didn't even mention me." Suzi whispered, drooping. "Not once."

"Suzanne!" Beverley said sharply. "How can you say that, when such a cruel article has just been written about our poor sister?"

Suzi went red. "I didn't mean to be unfeeling."

"She's right." Ava said, and her voice sounded faint to her own ears. "Nobody will be thinking about Suzi now. It was meant to be her first introduction to Society. She did so well, but if she isn't even mentioned in the scandal sheets, everybody will forget about her. I shouldn't be attracting all this attention."

Suzi turned to Lord Mortensen.

"Father, could we not take action? This is nothing but a collection of vile falsehoods. Assuredly..."

"These aren't like newspapers, my dear." He said heavily, shaking his head. "Did you see any names attached to the articles? They are written anonymously, all of them. They are printed secretly and given out throughout London. Judging by the information inside them, they are written by a member of the *Ton*, but it could really be anyone. After all, there were hundreds and hundreds of people at the ball last night. It could have been any one of them. There could be several writers, for all we know."

Ava stared down at the other sheets. There were a number of gossip columns written, some more popular than others. She could see at a glance that the scandal sheet with her article in it was the most popular one in London. Everyone would have read it by luncheon.

Everyone. Including...

Ava squeezed her eyes closed. She wanted to cry, but of course that would do nobody any good.

Had Lord Thame seen this article? If he had not, he would soon read it, or at least be told about it.

How would he react? Would he read it with growing horror, and put aside the magazine with a shudder, congratulating himself on a lucky escape? Maybe he would find it funny. Maybe he had been laughing at Ava behind his hands the whole time anyway.

Even if he thought hardly anything at all, one thing would be certain.

He would not be visiting today. The best thing for him to do in this case was to avoid her as determinedly as he could. After this article, the whole world would be watching them.

Watching Ava, particularly.

Ava glanced around the table, taking in the drawn, worried faces of her family. Beverley was clutching her stomach, and Ava prayed that the shock wouldn't disrupt the baby. Her mother's face was pale and pinched, and Suzi was staring down at the table. Ava's heart clenched.

Suzi had always hovered in the background. She was quieter than her siblings. She was not as beautiful as Beverley, or as studious and clever as Ava. But she was young and sweet-natured, and had looked forward to her coming out for longer than Ava could remember. She had been a flurry of nerves and excitement, expectant and hopeful.

And now her coming-out had been tainted. It was all about Ava, and Suzi was pushed to the sidelines once again.

Ava edged her hand across the table, making to take her sister's hand.

"Suzi…" she whispered.

Her sister glanced up at her, as if seeing her for the first time. She dropped her gaze at once, sliding her hand off the table and onto her lap.

Ava felt indisposed.

Somebody rapped forcefully on the door, causing them all to startle. They heard the door open, and heard the shuffle of a man's boots in the foyer.

"Who's that?" Beverley asked faintly. "It's far too early for guests."

Even though she knew it was a silly, silly mistake, Ava felt a spark of hope.

Maybe it was *him,* outraged at the ridiculous scandal sheet, come to tell her... tell her what?

They all turned to face the doorway, waiting. Ava held her breath.

Chapter Eight

Dominic was jerked awake from a perfectly pleasant dream to find Richard sitting in a chair beside his bed, prodding him with his walking-stick.

"Goodness gracious, you slumber like a person absconded from this earthly realm." Richard muttered disapprovingly.

Dominic dropped his face into his pillow. "And you have no sense of boundaries, my friend. How on earth did you get in here?"

"Peeves let me in. He likes me. Your valet doesn't seem to be up and about yet, so I thought I'd find you myself."

"Of course you did. What time is it?"

"Ten o' clock, I think."

"Well, no wonder he isn't up. It was half past one by the time I got to bed. What is so important that you had to wake me so early? Or did you simply fancy a little conversation?"

Richard's expression shifted, and Dominic's smile faded. He'd meant it as a joke, but it occurred to him for the first time that if Richard had come barging into his room like this, something was probably wrong.

"Richard? What is it?"

"You might want to give this a read." Richard remarked, tossing a newspaper onto Dominic's bed.

No, not a newspaper. A thin sort of magazine. It took a moment for Dominic to recognize it as one of the scandal sheets, the ludicrous gossip columns that circulated Society and were, for some reason, taken seriously.

"Why on earth are you giving me this nonsense? I never read these."

"Really? You should." Richard remarked, picking non-existent pieces of lint from the knee of his trousers. "They're ridiculous, of course, but even the most nonsensical stories have a kernel of truth. Such as the one on the front page, for example. Go on, read it."

Dominic did. He sat slowly up in bed, reading first in mild curiosity and then in growing horror.

The article focused on his conversation and dance with Lady Ava Devane the previous night. It had been an entirely normal interaction, of course, and one that – to him, at least – seemed full of promise. The author of the ridiculous scandal sheet portrayed Lady Ava as a scheming, conniving woman, bitter at her spinsterhood, trying to ensnare Dominic.

It clashed strongly with the Lady Ava he knew, who had struck him as intelligent, independent, and entirely content with herself.

"Who pens such drivel?" Dominic managed at last, flipping through the pages in an attempt to find some sort of explanation, some more information, *anything*.

There was nothing, of course, only dull accounts of parties, and small incidents blown up into 'scandals'.

A horrible thought occurred to him. "Do you think Lady Ava has read this?"

"Almost certainly. Most ladies read the scandal sheets whenever they come out, and certainly after a social event they have attended. If she hasn't read it already – which I doubt – she'll soon be informed of it."

Dominic scrambled out of bed, flinging on his robe.

"Well, we need to get this dealt with. We need to get this article removed, and a retraction and apology printed."

Richard chuckled. "One can tell that you don't read the scandal sheets often enough. They're anonymous."

Dominic wilted, sinking down onto the edge of his bed.

"What am I to do, then? This paints me as a ridiculous fool, and Lady Ava as a grasping harpy."

"Are you sure she is not? A grasping harpy, I mean."

He flinched. "Of course I am sure. I liked her very much."

Richard inspected the tip of his walking-stick. "I'm sure you did, but it pays to be careful, doesn't it?"

Dominic was not listening. As promised, Jasper had laid out fresh clothes for him – a daring blue-and-gold silk waistcoat, finer than anything Dominic would have chosen for himself, a fresh cravat with a note reading *Cravate en Cascade* left beside it. A pea-green coat and brown breeches were also set down, along with his freshly polished hessians.

"I can't wear this." Dominic muttered. "Blue and green? I'll look ridiculous."

"I don't know." Richard responded, tilting his head. "It may well work. That gentleman of yours is a clever fellow. Proceed, give it a try. Allow me to witness how proficient it is."

Dominic sighed, raking his fingers through his hair.

"Very well. Would it be too much to ask for you to wait downstairs, while I get a wash and shave? Ask Peeves to put on some breakfast for you."

"I believe he already has." Richard remarked, with just a hint of smugness.

***

Dominic heard the voices of his children before he reached the dining room door and suppressed a smile.

"I want a walking-stick when I'm grown up," he heard Steven announce. "With a gold tip like Uncle Richard."

He heard Richard chuckling. "Well, perhaps I'll keep mine for you to have, then."

Dominic shouldered open the door, and saw Richard perched on a dining room chair, the three children swinging off his arms. Emily stood nearby, smiling fondly.

"Ah, see, your Papa is here." Richard said, picking up little Maria and turning her around to see Dominic. The two older children gave squeals of delight and hurried to hug their father.

"Emily said that she is not angry with me." Daniella whispered in his ear. "But that I mustn't do it again."

Dominic dropped onto one knee, looking her seriously in the face.

"Emily is very kind, darling, and we will talk about this later, like grown-ups."

Daniella nodded, seeming pleased at the idea of doing anything *like a grown-up*. Dominic kissed her forehead and swept his son and youngest daughter into his arms.

"Now, don't you all think that your papa looks very charming?" Richard said, eyes glinting with mischief.

Steven and Maria clamoured to say *yes*, although Daniella fell silent. She eyed him with pursed lips, and Dominic wondered whether she suspected what he was doing.

No, surely not. She was only a child, after all.

Although it was fairly certain that Daniella would not initially be pleased with the prospect of a new mama. Not at first, at least.

Dominic swallowed hard.

Calm yourself, you're running away with yourself. So far, you are only going to Lady Ava's home to apologise, and nothing more.

He met Richard and Emily's eye over the heads of the children. Attentive as always, Emily stepped forward.

"Come on, children, time to go back to the nursery." She said, all cool affection. "We have lessons to do, and your papa has work to do."

"Can we have supper with papa tonight?" Daniella spoke up, glancing pleadingly between her father and her nurse.

Dominic scooped her into his arms, and she put her little arms around his neck, squeezing tight as if she were afraid to let go.

"We shall all eat supper together." He said firmly.

"Even Nurse Emily?" Steven chimed in.

"Of course Nurse Emily. We could not leave her out, could we? Now, you must all be good for Emily, and get on with your lessons, you will, won't you?"

They all insisted that they would be *extremely* good and were dutifully hustled out of the dining room by Emily, and the door closed behind them. Dominic stood for a moment, listening to the clamour of chattering and running footsteps leading back upstairs. He felt a painful ache inside him, reminding him that Marianne would never see their children grow.

"They are sweet children, Dominic." Richard said quietly. "But they need a mother. They need two parents – they're too difficult to manage otherwise."

"Are you calling my children difficult, Richard?"

"No, I'm calling them *children*. You know I'm right."

Dominic sat heavily in one of the dining room chairs, and eyed the breakfast spread. His appetite was gone.

"I do know. I worry that I'm going to let them down, you know. And Marianne, while I'm at it."

"You're doing your best." Richard remarked, his voice low. "Nobody can ask for more."

"Of course they can. What if my best isn't good enough?" Dominic swallowed hard, closing his eyes. "I've been thinking, you know. About Lady Ava. That scandal sheet story is nonsense, of course, and the more I think about her, the more I think that maybe… maybe she is the sort of woman I've been looking for."

Richard absorbed this, nodding slowly. "And you think she'd be amenable? To a marriage of convenience, that is?"

"I don't know. I hope so. I suppose I'll only find out when I ask her, won't I? Nevertheless, prior to any other matters, I must pay her a visit and offer my sincerest apologies regarding the aforementioned article."

"Apologise? Why? You didn't do anything. You had nothing to do with it."

Dominic fidgeted. "No, but I daresay she must be becoming quite fervent about it. It was not flattering."

"Not in the slightest, no. But I ought to say something – let her know that I don't agree with it, and I will tell everyone I meet that it's an utter balderdash. I think she deserves a little reassurance, at least."

Richard nodded, and Dominic worked up the courage to say what he meant to say next.

"And I think it will make her more amenable to my proposal."

Richard lifted an eyebrow. "Why, because she has no other choice?"

"No, of course not! Don't be awful, Richard. I mean because she is tired of Society, and tired of them making fun of her. I can give her status.I shall prove them wrong and force them to consume their own disparaging speech regarding her."

"Revenge, then."

"That's a harsh word, Richard. But yes, more or less. I can give her revenge. I can give the scandal sheets something to really talk about."

Richard chuckled. "Oh, now that *is* exciting."

Chapter Nine

Ava's heart pounded.

Please let it be him, she prayed, even as she realized how silly it was to hope such a thing.

Then the door to the dining room opened, and Gordon came storming in.

All hope was immediately crushed, and Ava couldn't quite suppress a little gasp of disappointment.

"Gordon, it's you. So early in the morning, too." Lady Mortensen said faintly, and Ava suspected that her mother had held similar hopes, too.

"Indeed, I was unable to attain slumber with these nonsensical rumours circulating." Gordon snapped, tossing a crumpled copy of the same scandal sheet onto the table. It looked as though he'd thrown it on the floor and stamped on it. "Have you read it?"

"Of course we have read it, Gordon." Lord Mortensen rumbled. "Don't stamp around, if you please. Sit down, and we shall discuss this like adults."

Gordon huffed, but obeyed, moving over to sit beside Ava. He reached out, giving her hand a quick, reassuring squeeze.

"We'll sort this out at once, Ava." He said quietly. It was meant to console her, but Ava couldn't help feeling as if there was just another barrier between Suzi and her now.

Suzi hadn't said a word, not since she'd been accused of being unfeeling. She sat hunched over in her seat, staring down at the table.

"We must consider the restoration of our reputation." Lady Mortensen remarked resolutely.

"Should we send Ava to the country?" Gordon suggested.

"Absolutely not. That would be tantamount to admitting every accusation."

"But that's hardly fair. She can't be expected to..."

They broke out into conversation, everyone talking over everyone else. Ava leaned back in her seat, drawing in long, deep breaths, and willing herself to stay calm.

Suzi got up abruptly, murmuring something about needing

some air, and slipped away from the table. Nobody noticed, and the conversation didn't even dip.

Ava noticed, of course. She watched her sister disappear into the hall, closing the door behind her. On impulse, she bounced up from the table, and went to follow her.

"Where are you going, Ava?" Beverley demanded sharply.

"It's too hot in here. I'll just be a moment. Go on, keep talking."

They did. She heard the conversation resume behind her, and Ava set herself hurrying down the hallway, after the hem of Suzi's disappearing skirts.

Suzi went to the morning-room, her favourite room in the house. It was a pleasant place, suitably formal for entertaining but not stuffy, with clean, white walls, tasteful decorations, and plenty of light. When Ava let herself in after her sister, she found her settling down in the window seat, her face turned away from the room.

"Suzi?" Ava spoke quietly.

"I'd like to be alone, Ava."

"You're angry with me."

Suzi shook her head. "I'm not unfeeling, Ava, truly I'm not. This is awful for you, I know that, it's just..." she trailed off. "No. I won't be called selfish."

Ava crossed the room, perching at the other end of the window seat.

"You are not selfish to want one night to yourself." She said fiercely. "The ball last night was *your* coming out. It was meant to be all about you – we all intended it that way. It was your moment, and you deserve it."

Suzi was crying, Ava could see that. Tear stains streaked down her cheek, and dripped off the edge of her chin.

"I'm so tired of being forgotten." She whispered. "I love you so much, Ava – and Gordon, and Beverley, even when she's being pernickety. I love you all, but I know that next to the three of you I'm dull and boring."

"You are nothing of the sort. We would all fight somebody who said that you were."

"In comparison you all, I mean. And last night, I felt so *good* about myself. I don't need to be the centre of attention, but I looked beautiful, and I felt comfortable in my skin, and I made friends that were *mine*, and gentlemen admired me... oh, I know it's shallow, but I loved it all so much. And my siblings were there too, and my parents, and you were all proud of me, and I was just perfectly happy. I was so excited for the rest of my Season. But now, all anyone will talk about is you."

She shook her head, biting her lip. "I know it's awful, Ava, and I should be more sympathetic, but... are you angry at me?"

"I could never be angry at you for speaking your mind." Ava said firmly, taking her sister's hand. "I worked so hard not to embarrass you last night. I truly did. I have jeopardised your prospects, plain and simple. I'm sorry, Suzi, I'm so sorry."

Suzi wiped her eyes with the back of her hand and threw her arms around Ava.

"I'm not angry at *you*, not even at the others. I know that this isn't your fault. I don't even know who I'm angry at – beyond the writer of that wretched scandal sheet, of course – but I don't know what to do."

"First of all, we need to discuss..." Ava's firm voice faded. She cocked her head, listening. No, it was not her imagination. Those really were carriage wheels making their way up the drive.

Suzi pressed her cheek to the window, where she had a good view down the drive, all the way to the iron gates at the bottom.

"There's a chaise coming up." She said, voice hushed. "I can't make out the crest on the side. Oh..." she sucked in a sharp breath, eyes widening. "It's Lord Thame's carriage."

***

Lord Thame stood in the parlour, gloves in his hand, looking thoroughly uncomfortable. He was faced by almost the entire Devane family – Lord and Lady Mortensen, Beverley, Gordon, Ava, and Suzi.

There was a brief moment of tension after the usual pleasantries had been exchanged.

"I must say..."

"I suppose you came about..."

Both Ava and Lord Thame spoke at the same time, and both flushed and fell silent.

"You first." Lord Thame said.

"No, I insist."

"*I* insist."

"It's my house."

He swallowed. "Very well. I came about that ludicrous article in the scandal sheets. I assume you have read it?"

Ava closed her eyes briefly. "Yes, I have. I was deeply upset, as you can imagine."

"As was I. It portrayed both of us in an unfair, deeply unflattering light. You as a scheming harpy, and me as a bone-headed simpleton. I was outraged on your behalf, and on mine."

She let out a breath, and a knot of tension loosened in her chest.

"I am glad that you did not…" she faltered, not sure that she wanted to continue.

He lifted a wry eyebrow. "Did not what? Did not believe those nonsensical lies about you? I certainly gave them no credence, not at all. You must have a very low opinion of me, Lady Ava."

Ava flushed, struggling to think of what to say next.

Fortunately, her mother came to her rescue.

"We're all rather shaken, as you can imagine, Lord Thame." Lady Mortensen interjected. "As you likely know, last night was my youngest daughter's first outing into Society, which has now been quite overshadowed by all this nonsense. I'm sure you can appreciate that none of us are thinking straight."

"Of course, of course." Lord Thame demurred. "I came here at once to assure you – all of you – that I am as outraged at this as you, and I have no intention of curtailing our growing acquaintanceship."

There was a taut silence at that. Ava could almost sense her mother's hopes rising.

"Well, I am glad to hear that. Very glad." Lady Mortensen said breathlessly. "There are some honourable gentlemen left in Society after all, it seems. Suzi, ring the bell for tea. You will stay for tea, won't you, Lord Thame?"

He shifted, looking a little ill at ease. Nervous, Ava would have said.

"Usually, I would gladly stay, but in fact I wondered if I might speak privately with Lady Ava."

The atmosphere seemed to get tighter and more expectant. Ava could have sworn that she couldn't breathe.

"Oh?" Beverley said giddily. "Now, you mean?"

Lord Thame swallowed audibly. "That is to say, I was wondering if Lady Ava would care to accompany me out on a chaise ride in the Park. It's not the fashionable hour, of course, but I prefer quieter times."

They all looked at Ava, all willing her to accept.

Ava's mouth was dry.

Stop running away with your imagination, she told herself firmly. *He's probably going to awkwardly tell you that he has no interest but doesn't want to appear weak under Society's scrutiny, so we must pretend to be friends.*

It would be easier to say no, to stay here and console Suzi, and to somehow claw back her shredded reputation. There must, after all, be *something* she could do.

"Of course." Ava heard herself say. "I should love to."

***

Lord Thame's chaise was a very fine one, as was to be expected. It was a jaunty yellow, almost matching Ava's plain ruffled dress – mostly covered up by a more sedate travelling cloak – and had been recently painted and lacquered.

The Devanes preferred more practical vehicles, so their usual carriage was a large, sturdy one, with a roof and coachman, well-sprung and sensible.

Apparently, Lord Thame felt otherwise.

The chaise had an open roof, which could be put up in bad weather. Today was not bad weather, so Ava found herself open to the elements. Lord Thame had no coachman, preferring instead to manage his two sleek-flanked horses himself. The chaise was higher than she was used to, and it was odd to be so exposed.

The wind raked through her hair, and Ava tried not to notice people staring as they went by.

Had she ever gone out with a gentleman in his chaise? No, she had not. She had only been in a chaise a handful of times, and always in drizzling rain with the roof up, never sitting beside her driver like this.

Lizzie was here, of course, but she sat in the back, alone. What was more, Ava knew that her maid could not hear a word over the rushing of the wind past their ears.

They took a sharp turn into the Park, and Lord Thame was obliged to slow his rocketing pace. Ava breathed a sigh of relief.

He smiled wryly at her, no doubt noticing.

"I beg your pardon, Lady Ava. Was I driving too fast?"

"It is your chaise. You can drive as fast or as slow as you like."

He chuckled, shaking his head. "That awful article has driven a wedge between us, I fear."

She felt herself relax, just a little. "I am glad that your opinion of me has not changed."

"Nor yours of me, I hope. I would never believe such nonsense."

Ava was beginning to feel foolish, thinking that a man as sensible as Lord Thame would give the scandal sheets even a moment's thought. Had he brought her out here to apologize privately?

"I suppose you are wondering why I invited you to drive in the Park, at such an early and unfashionable hour." Lord Thame said suddenly, as if he'd been reading her thoughts.

She shifted in her seat. "I was, rather, yes. You must know that this will only inflame the gossip about us."

"I know that, yes. The truth is – and I shall flatter you by speaking plainly, as plainly as I can – that I have a proposal for you."

A proposal. Ava's heart hammered against her chest.

It couldn't be the type of proposal she was thinking of. Not even the most foolish romantics would propose to a woman after one conversation and one dance. And no woman of any sense would accept, either.

She glanced over her shoulder, and found that Lizzie was absorbed in a book, paying no attention to them at all.

"Pray, continue." She said, her voice sounding somewhat distant. "What proposal is this?"

He was quiet for a moment or two, seemingly concentrating on managing the reins.

"I mentioned that I was widowed, Lady Ava."

"You did, yes. Again, my condolences."

"My wife has been dead for two years. Our marriage was not, initially, based on love, but rather compatibility and mutual friendship. I was extremely happy with her, and flatter myself that I made her happy, too. Just before she died, she urged me to marry again. She did not want me to be alone, she said, and felt that the children needed a mother."

Ava went very still. "It sounds like a fortuitous arrangement." She heard herself say.

A marriage of convenience. That was what it had been.

"It was." Lord Thame said, eyes still fixed on the road ahead. "As you can imagine, I took the task of finding a new companion very seriously. In short, I am here this Season to marry again. I would like to marry you, Lady Ava."

The declaration, when it came, was so simple and frank that Ava almost missed it. She flinched, blinking rapidly as the full meaning of his words sank in.

"You want to marry me?" she said slowly. "Regardless of the scandal sheet article?"

He winced. "That hurried on my proposal somewhat. I suppose I was afraid you would abscond to the country or refuse to see me again."

She stared at him for a long moment, until he cleared his throat uncomfortably.

"Well, Lady Ava? What do you say?"

A flash of rage and disappointment rushed through her.

"You are making fun of me." Ava said, teeth gritted.

Lord Thame glanced down at her, eyes wide. "What? I assure you..."

"Is it a wager, perhaps? A bet? Or simply a joke to you?"

"I would never..."

"Stop the carriage, Lord Thame, I would like to get out."

"Lady Ava, please..."

Regardless of the distance her seat stood above the floor, or the speed at which the carriage was going, Ava got to her feet.

"Stop the carriage at *once*!"

He hauled on the reins, and the carriage lurched to a shuddering stop that nearly threw Ava down. She maintained her balance and began at once to navigate the climb down to the ground.

"Milady?" Lizzie called uncertainly, leaning forward. "What is it?"

"We are walking home, Lizzie." Ava called back, wondering if she dared risk a broken ankle and leap down from the seat. Flustered, Lizzie began to fiddle with the chaise door.

In a flash, Lord Thame had slid across the seat, and grabbed her wrist.

Ava froze.

He was wearing delicate kid gloves, ideal for riding, and the soft material felt luxurious against her bare skin. His fingers circled around her wrist, between the end of her cuff and the beginning of her glove. His grip was firm but not tight. She could wrench her arm away whenever she liked; it was a grip designed to get her attention rather than keep her still.

She did not wrench her arm away. She should have done, of course, as it was a gross impropriety. The touch sent shivers down her arm.

"Please, Lady Ava." Lord Thame said quietly, eyes pleading at her. "I am not making fun of you. I swear on the lives of my children that my proposal is genuine."

Ava swallowed thickly. He released her wrist with a start, as if he hadn't realized what he was doing, and shuffled back to his seat, waiting for her decision.

It would be silly to get out and walk home from the middle of the Park, anyway. Ava hauled herself back into the seat, shaking out her skirts somewhat self-consciously.

Thank goodness it wasn't the fashionable hour, and there were not many people around to see.

"Milady?" Lizzie asked tentatively. "Are we getting out?"

"No, Lizzie." Ava responded shortly. "We are not getting out. Drive on, Lord Thame, please."

He wordlessly snapped the reins, and the horses pulled away again. Ava closed her eyes, willing her breathing to return to normal.

"I did not mean to offend you." Lord Thame said, after a few minutes. "And truly, I am not mocking you in any way. I am not a man to enjoy such cruelty or make such jokes – if one could call them jokes, of course."

"I was wrong to accuse you of doing so." She said quietly. "I am sorry."

He was looking at her, she knew, watching her closely. Ava did not look at him, keeping her eyes on the horses' backs instead.

"If my proposal offends you in any way, please, say the word, and I will stop talking about it at once." He said, his voice low and sincere. "I meant what I said. I believe I can offer you a comfortable and happy life as Lady Thame. You will have status, money, power, and freedom. I will never get in the way of your studies or of the way you wish to conduct your life, so long as you can be a true partner to me and help me with my children. They are of paramount concern to me."

She swallowed hard. "It... it is a surprising proposal." She admitted.

"Yes, it is. I am sorry."

"There is nothing to forgive. May I think it over?"

"Of course, of course."

They drove on in silence for another moment, until Ava summoned up the courage to ask him to take her home.

Wordlessly, he obeyed.

Chapter Ten

"I don't think you handled that well, Dominic." Richard remarked, eyes on his cards.

Dominic sighed. "Thank you, Richard, that's most helpful."

"I wasn't trying to be helpful. It's your turn, by the way."

Dominic played his hand, although his mind wasn't on the game, not one bit.

They'd met at the club, and Dominic had reluctantly told Richard the whole business with Lady Ava. She hadn't spoken at all to him about the proposal he made, and they'd parted ways without mentioning it at all.

"Do you think I offended her?" Dominic asked, after a pause.

Richard sighed, throwing down his cards. He'd won, anyway. Nobody ever managed to beat Richard at cards, or chess, or any sort of game.

"I don't know. It's not a ridiculous proposal – most gentlemen and ladies marry without any real affection. But to be so blunt about it might have shaken her sensibilities."

"I don't think Lady Ava is the sort of lady to quibble over *sensibilities.*"

"You don't know that." Richard pointed out. "You *hope* that, but it's not at all the same thing."

"That's right," Dominic responded heavily. "Oh, truly, what have I done?"

Before Richard could speak again, a gold-liveried footman appeared at Dominic's elbow, a silver platter resting on one gloved palm, a neat, folded piece of paper on the platter.

Dominic took the paper, read it through, and grimaced.

Richard lifted his eyebrows. "Not good news, I assume."

"No. My father-in-law has arrived. Forgive me, but I'd better get home."

Richard winced. "No forgiveness needed. Go, please. I don't envy you."

***

His Grace George Beaumont, the Duke of Mertonshire, was a

man who'd experienced loss.

Or so the scandal sheets claimed. He was a widower and had lost his only daughter in tragic circumstances. Forced to stand at a distance, he yearned for the love of his grandchildren, and offered fatherly advice and timeless wisdom to his struggling son-in-law.

Of course, Dominic knew that was nonsense.

His father-in-law had made himself comfortable in Dominic's study, taking the largest, most comfortable armchair and holding out one booted foot to the fire.

He barely glanced up as Dominic entered, leaving him feeling like the guest, instead of the master of the house.

"I had the children put to bed," the Duke said absently.

"It's too early for them to go to bed," Dominic responded, surprised.

"They ought to be in bed by now."

"It is too early."

The Duke sighed, as if Dominic were just as troublesome as the children. "Well, I sent them to bed. I wish you would see that things were done properly here, Dominic. Just because Marianne is gone does not mean that our standards can slip. By the by, Daniella was displeased at going to bed, and ran off somewhere. You'd better find her."

Dominic took in a few deep breaths to steady himself. Whenever his father-in-law visited – never announced, and always with plenty of unwanted advice to give – the household seemed to turn upside down.

"Very well. Do help yourself to whiskey, George."

"I already have," he said, lifting a half-empty glass with a hint of irritation, as if Dominic was the one who was taking liberties.

Swallowing his annoyance, Dominic turned to leave.

***

Emily had, thankfully, seen where Daniella had gone. It was a relief to know where she was, although where she had gone worried Dominic.

He pushed open the door to Lady Thame's long abandoned bedroom and was immediately struck by the chill of the room.

Daniella had crawled onto the bed and sat there, cross-legged, the silken bedspread rumpling around her.

Dominic took a moment to compose himself, trying to swallow down the lump in his throat.

The room was kept just as Marianne had left it, with an occasional dusting and airing to prevent it from getting musty.

"Emily said you'd come up here," Dominic said carefully. "What's the matter, dearest?"

"Grandpapa put us to bed too early," Daniella murmured. "I'm allowed to stay up a bit later, aren't I, Papa?"

"That is right, dearest."

Taking a breath, Dominic made himself cross the room, boots sinking into the deep-pile carpet. These apartments had been resolutely Marianne's, decorated just how she wanted, and he rarely ventured inside. It felt odd to be in here now.

He perched on the edge of the bed, the slippery bedspread shifting underneath him. It was gloomy in here, but he could see Daniella's large eyes glittering in the dark, fixed on him.

"I'm sorry that Grandpapa made you go to bed early," Dominic said quietly, after a pause. "I should have been here to tell him otherwise. He only wants the best for you, you know. He misses your Mamma."

Daniella swallowed. "I know, he said so. What if I don't grow up like Mamma, though? Will he not like me?"

"Of course he will, and *I* will. Your mamma loved you, you know that, no matter what you did." He shuffled closer, putting an arm around Daniella, and pulling her close. She sagged against him, tiny cold hands slipping around his waist. He would have to get her to bed soon, buried in her quilts, with the fire blazing nicely in the nursery fireplace.

"What if you die, like Mamma did?" Daniella said quietly, so quietly that he almost missed it.

Dominic kissed the top of her head. "I won't die, darling."

She pulled away, looking him full in the face. "How do you *know*? You *might* die. I've been thinking about it a lot. And if you do die, then what will happen to the little ones and me? I'll be all by myself. You will be gone, *and* Mamma, and I don't think that I can stand for it."

Dominic's breath caught in his throat. "I won't die, I promise."

73

"You can't promise." A few tears were glittering in Daniella's eyes now. "I'm not a *baby*, Papa. I know that you didn't mean for Mamma to die, and everyone says that it's a horrible tragedy and wasn't supposed to happen, and so that means you can't do anything about it. You *could* die."

Dominic opened his mouth, intending to say something calm and reassuring. Of course, nothing came to mind. Of course not. What could a person say to convince a child that mortality was nothing to be afraid of? Frankly, it *was* something to fear.

He didn't intend to die but promising that he would *not* die was simply something he couldn't do, and Daniella had the sense to point this out.

Swallowing hard, he wrapped his arms around the little girl and held her close.

"I am not going anywhere, darling," he said quietly. "And even if something were to happen to me, your siblings and you would not be left alone. I can promise you that."

Daniella sniffled, seeming somewhat mollified. She huddled against her father, wiping her nose with the back of his hand.

"Perhaps," Dominic continued, hesitantly, "A new Mamma would make you feel better."

That was the wrong thing to say. Daniella moved back at once, eyes wide with outrage.

"A new mamma?" she gasped. "Oh, no."

Dominic tried to salvage the situation. "I don't mean to replace your real mamma, of course, just..."

"I don't want a new mamma," Daniella said defiantly, sliding to the ground. "I *don't*."

She scuttled across the floor towards the cracked-open doorway, light from the hallway spilling into the room. Dominic was left curled awkwardly up in the bed, feeling out of place and remarkably foolish.

Outside, he heard Emily talking gently to Daniella, then the nurse poked her head into the room.

"I shall take Miss Daniella to bed, sir," she said lightly, and Dominic nodded.

"Thank you, Emily."

***

74

The Duke sat in the armchair in front of the fire, as if he hadn't moved an inch since Dominic had gone.

Well, perhaps he hadn't.

"Is the girl mollified?" the Duke spoke at last, not tearing his eyes away from the dancing flames.

"Daniella is in bed, yes," Dominic said curtly, pouring himself a generous splash of brandy. "She's over-tired, I think."

"Hm. She's getting harder and harder to manage as she grows. Children are troublesome, you know. Young parents think that raising children is a walk in the park, and it is not."

Dominic bit his lip. "I'm sure most parents know the challenges that child-rearing brings," he responded placidly.

The Duke seemed not to have heard him. Lifting the toe of his boot, the man inspected his highly polished Hessians with complacency.

"How is your wife-search coming along?" he asked, just as Dominic was settling himself into the seat opposite.

The question made Dominic flinch, but he forced himself not to snap back a response.

Instead, he settled himself as comfortably as possible, and took a long sip of his brandy.

"I do believe that a stepmother will be a good thing for the children," he said lightly. "And I am searching for a woman who would be the right fit. It's not easy, you know."

The Duke sniffed. "Nonsense. You can't possibly be trying hard enough. Marianne gave you her blessing to remarry, did she not? New debutantes are coming out all the time."

"I don't particularly want to marry an eighteen-year-old girl. I want a grown woman, maybe even a widow with children of her own, someone who will be a good fit for my family and me."

The Duke pursed his lips. Perhaps he'd half-expected an angry denial, an insistence that he, Dominic, would not remarry. In the first year after Marianne's death, Dominic had taken any suggestions of remarriage as a personal insult. The Duke and he had engaged in altercations on multiple occasions.

Now, they had reached an uneasy sort of peace. The Duke didn't meddle in Dominic's affairs more than was absolutely necessary and had at least stopped trying to trap him into marriage with various ladies.

The man sighed, draining his glass of whiskey. Dominic watched him, not quite trusting himself to relax. He wished his father-in-law would go home.

Little chance of that, though.

"Children need two parents," he said at last. "I pity those who raise children alone for whatever reason, and I am sure they do their best. Perhaps with only one child, that might be managed, but if there is more than one – well. Children require a great deal of time, attention, and care to be properly raised. Far more than most people understand. I do not see how the business can be accomplished with only one parent. You are a diligent father, Dominic, I bestow you that accolade, and a good husband to my Marianne. I know you have their interests at heart, and I trust you will believe that *I* have *your* interests at heart when I tell you that you should marry and marry soon."

Dominic swallowed. "I am trying, believe it or not. But I think that marrying the wrong woman will be just as detrimental to my children as not marrying at all. Perhaps more so."

"Perhaps. But listen to this, Dominic. I raised a daughter myself, and I know the difficulties girls present. Society would have us believe that females are dull, empty-headed creatures, but you and I know that is not the case. Already, Daniella is coming into her own. She has questions about her mother's death, about her own mortality, and so on. She is a discerning young lady and will likely perceive the disparities Society presents between herself and her sister, as well as their brother."

"I know, and I can guide her through it."

"Perhaps. I don't doubt your enthusiasm. But, Dominic, ladies need their mothers. A female influence on Daniella, and later Maria, is very necessary."

"I mentioned a new mamma to Daniella only half an hour ago, and she resisted it in the strongest terms."

The Duke sighed again. He looked tired now, sagging lower and lower into his chair, the glass hanging loose from his fingers. Dominic wanted to lean forward and take the glass, setting it safely down on the coffee table. He might have done it, too, if it wouldn't have offended his father-in-law.

"The older she gets, the more unpleasant the idea of a

76

stepmother will become. Believe me, Daniella is of the age where she can still be happy with the idea of a stepmother. Choose wisely, and you will marry a woman who will improve your life and the lives of your children."

"And what of her life?"

The Duke blinked, taken aback. "Well, she will have a family and a house. What more could a woman want?"

"That is hardly fair."

The Duke sniffed, finally setting down his empty glass. "That is beside the point. Have you *any* women in mind this Season?"

Dominic bit his lip. He had no intention of baring his heart to his father-in-law, of course, but it wouldn't hurt to say *something*.

"There is a lady I like," he admitted tightly.

The Duke gave a grunt and a nod, seeking no more details. "Good. Sooner rather than later, my boy. Believe me on that. Sooner rather than later."

He rose to his feet, and Dominic automatically rose too.

"It must be dark outside," he said, setting aside his brandy. "Why don't you stay the night? I can have a spare room made up for you at once."

The Duke smiled wryly. "Such a dutiful son-in-law. You're a good father, Dominic. Don't let anyone tell you otherwise."

Dominic suppressed a smile. "They don't."

The Duke chuckled at that and took his leave. The offer of an overnight stay had clearly been rejected.

Dominic stood at the study window and watched his father-in-law's carriage rumble down the drive.

Now all he could do was wait for Ava to write back to him and pray that her response was favourable.

Chapter Eleven

"I haven't told anyone. Not a soul. Not even Suzi," Ava confessed, and it felt like a great weight off her chest. She reached forward for her cup of tea, which had almost gone cold in the time it had taken to explain the situation to Willi and gulped it eagerly.

Willi, who'd scarcely moved during the whole story, let out a ragged sigh and leaned back in her seat.

"Well," she said at last, "that was unexpected. Are you sure it wasn't an ordinary proposal of marriage? Gentlemen can be a little nervous, and sometimes say the wrong thing."

Ava shook her head. "No, it was a marriage of convenience, plain and simple. I was rather glad to have it all laid out in such straightforward terms, you know? It made things easier."

Willi considered this, thoughtfully pursing her lips. "And you haven't told anyone? Not even your Mama?"

"No, I didn't. I... I know that they'd only want the best for me, and they think that getting married is the way to achieve that, so they would tell me to accept. I want to hear other advice."

Willi arched an eyebrow. "And what if there isn't any other advice?"

There was a pause between them. Ava swallowed hard, lifting her chin.

"What do you mean?"

Her friend sighed. "I think you know what I mean. You are twenty-six years old, and the only thing a twenty-six-year-old is permitted to do in our Society is to get married."

"I know *that*. I'm not a fool, Willi."

"I didn't say you were," she answered patiently, reaching for her own tea.

They were having afternoon tea in a fashionable little shop in the popular part of London, which served ices and cakes along with exotic teas and some rather good coffee. It was expensive, but the tables were widely spaced and there was plenty of privacy. In fact, Ava and Willi were lucky enough to have a booth, which protected them from prying eyes and listening ears, all at once.

"Let us go back to the beginning," Willi said, matter-of-factly. "How was his address? Was he hurried, brusque, absent-minded, or perhaps a little impolite? What was his manner like?"

"Slow down, Willi, please. I thought he was a *little* nervous, but it was all done properly and fairly. I never felt uncomfortable or upset, just... just taken aback."

"Understandable. I wouldn't say that he had shown a *marked interest*, nothing to warn you that he was thinking of making a proposal. And it's *de rigueur* to make a pretence of affection before a proposal, even if one has mercenary matters at heart."

Ava sighed. "You are a true romantic, Willi."

"I certainly hope not. Romance is all very well, but sometimes it's good to think of practicality."

They fell silent as the waiter approached, deftly refilling their teacups and placing another delicate plate of finger-cakes and small sandwiches on the table. He melted away, although the conversation didn't immediately pick up again.

"This is not the first proposal you've received," Willi said, speaking first. "But it is the first one that seems to have bothered you so much. And the first one you've asked for my advice on."

Ava smiled wryly. "Now that I'm a poor old spinster, the men are getting tired of me. What a shame."

"I can almost hear the dismay in your voice. But Lord Thame is a decent man, is he not? He's kind, and loves his children, and is well-spoken of all over London. Do you not think that such a man would make you happy?"

Ava swallowed hard, staring down into the amber depths of her tea. It tasted bitter, all of a sudden, as if her tongue had gone too dry to taste it. She didn't touch the finger-cakes and sandwiches on the plate – they would taste like sawdust in her mouth, she was sure of it.

Willi didn't push the plate towards her, but absently took a finger-cake for herself, chewing it thoughtfully.

"Do you like him, Ava?"

Ava flinched. "What does that have to do with anything?"

Her friend smiled wryly. "I would say that it has everything to do with all of it. If you like him..."

"It does not matter if I like him, as he is proposing a marriage of convenience and purely mercenary interests."

"Then," Willi said, setting down her teacup with a *clack*, "I suggest you consider some mercenary interests of your own."

"And why do I get the feeling that you have some ideas as to what those might be?"

"You would be correct," Willi affirmed, leaning forward and resting her elbows on the table in a way which would make her mother squawk with horror.

"Pray, do enlighten me, then."

Willi drew in a breath. "First of all, he's a personable gentleman. Not that it counts for much, but he is handsome, charming, and pleasant to be around. He's rich, of course. Secondly, a marriage like this would give you *status*. You know how unmarried women are treated – we're jokes, annoyances, something to be ignored when we stop being young and beautiful. Even if we have money, we're considered nuisances and expected to go and hide ourselves away in the countryside." Willi was obliged to take a pause to breathe, and Ava smiled wryly and sipped her tea.

"I agree. So, those are two concerns. A handsome husband to care for me, along with status and wealth. Anything else."

"Well, the way would be clear for Suzi to go about her Seasons."

Ava's smile disappeared. Willi hadn't meant to be unkind, of course she hadn't, but her comment had struck a nerve even so. Ava was doing her best not to embarrass her sister, but an older, unmarried sister was never going to be anything *but* an embarrassment.

Frankly, Ava was tired of her very existence being embarrassing, but she had to remember Suzi. Suzi deserved a future. She deserved a chance.

Ava shifted in her seat, clearing her throat.

"That is a point, although I would have to be careful that my engagement and marriage did not overshadow Suzi's first Season."

"Naturally. Oh, and there is one final thing to consider. You might end up with a family. I know that you like children."

"He has three children," Ava agreed. "I *would* have a family."

"Of course, but also you might have children of your own."

Ava flinched, straightening up. "It is not going to be *that* kind of marriage, Willi. It's all about convenience. He was clear on that. He wants a wife, a partner, a mother for his children."

"Well, perhaps it's time for you to think about what *you* want out of the marriage." Willi commented drily. "That is, if you intend to accept him."

There was a long pause between the two of them. Ava drained her cup of tea in deep, unladylike gulps, and rose to her feet.

"You've given me a great deal to think about, Willi. Thank you for all your advice."

Willi inclined her head. "Pray, do permit me to deliver you safely to your abode? I have had the carriage prepared for this very purpose."

"Thank you, but I think I'd rather walk. I need to clear my head. I suppose I have a weighty decision to make, and I'd better make it soon."

Her friend nodded, and Ava made her way across the tearoom floor, murmurs of conversation drifting up all around her. All of them, chatting of the past, the present, and the future, and all the while Ava's world was caving in.

She had to make a decision, but what if it were the wrong one? What if she found herself here again in five years' time, wishing desperately that she had accepted the Marquess?

Then again, what if she accepted him, and it turned out to be a huge mistake?

One thing is sure, she thought miserably to herself. *I can't go on as I have been.*

***

To His Lordship the Marquess of Thame, Lord Dominic Broughton

I extend my deepest appreciation for the delightful carriage ride through the Park, which we so thoroughly relished but a mere day prior. My compliments to you and your accomplished driving. Of course, I am not writing to you today in order to discuss your driving, nor to hint at another Promenade. I am writing in the relation to the matter we discussed during that drive, which was, in short, a proposal of marriage.

I am grateful for the time you so freely gave to me to think it over, and I am now ready to communicate my decision with you – let us hope the contents of this letter are to your liking.

If the subject was misunderstood, or your sentiments have changed, do write back immediately and tell me so – I shall not hold you to anything you said, nor any promises you made.

If your sentiments are unchanged, then I would like to gladly accept your offer of marriage. I do hope that our union brings satisfaction and peace to all involved, and I look forward with great interest to meeting your three dear children, of whom you are clearly so fond.

I believe that you and I have a great deal in common, and that we both have excellent qualities and attitudes to bring to a relationship which would benefit all involved – your children especially. I look forward to our partnership, and while we of course have some details to discuss in greater depth, I believe this is a fine start.

A response to this note would be greatly appreciated, so that we further discuss the matter. May I suggest another jaunt in the Park at the Fashionable Hour tomorrow, where we can freely discuss this matter. Do write back and advise.

Your Friend,
The Right Honourable Lady Ava Devane

PS. I am not sure if I conveyed my appreciation for your openness during the discussion we had in the Park, so let me so do here. It is refreshing to hear a matter properly discussed with clarity and frankness. So, thank you.

PPS. I have not mentioned our engagement – and the terms of our engagement – to my parents. This is something we can discuss soon enough, but I would be grateful if you do not mention this matter to them. Not yet, at least. My family believe that I am set upon spinsterhood. Also, I do not wish to overshadow my younger sister's Season, and after such a long period of singleness, I imagine that my engagement will cause quite a stir in the gossip columns and in general talk. I hope this does not bother you. If it does, then please do tell me at once. I would like to continue our relationship in the same manner in which it started – in a spirit of *honesty and frankness.*

***

To the Right Honourable Lady Ava Devane

I was delighted to receive your letter earlier this afternoon. I am glad for your speedy response to my proposal and sat down immediately to write a response.

Let me assure you at once that my sentiments have not changed, and I am keen to speed our engagement along relatively quickly, if that meets with your approval.

I am more than happy to meet in the Park at the fashionable hour, and we may take a walk around and discuss our business. You are a clever woman and I am sure you have considered this already, but might I suggest making a list of your demands/requirements, so that we can discuss each one in an organized manner? I am keen to fulfil your hopes as a husband and I am keen to provide you with a happy home and comfortable family life.

I am keen to introduce you to my children, and I am sure you will all get along famously. I shall tell you more about them when we meet. If I receive no note to the contrary, I shall assume that we will meet at the gateway to the Park at the time agreed.

Until then, accept my Fondest Wishes and Compliments
The Marquess of Thame, Lord Dominic Broughton

PS. I am glad that my openness did not offend you. I was concerned that you would find it over-forward and distasteful. I must admit that I am relieved at your desire for honesty and frankness in our relationship.

PPS. I will wait until you give me the word to mention our engagement to your parents. I will of course seek your parents' blessing and permission, although I am aware that you are of age, and it is your agreement which concerns me most of all. I have no desire to overshadow your dear sister's Season and will comply with whatever measures you feel necessary. Once again, we may discuss this tomorrow.

Chapter Twelve

He was there.

Ava had half-expected Lord Thame not to meet her at the gates to the Park, as if it were all some ridiculous joke.

Would I have been relieved, or disappointed? She thought. It was hard to tell, really.

He was dressed neatly, in a deep emerald-green walking coat, with top hat and cane, and shiny Hessian boots. He was pacing up and down in front of the entrance, head down, seemingly engrossed in his thoughts.

She was almost in front of him when he finally looked up, and she was sure she saw a flash of apprehension and relief on his face.

Had he wondered whether *she* would show up? Probably.

"Lord Thame," Ava said politely. "You are very punctual."

"So are you. I see that you brought your maid?"

"Yes, I thought it would be appropriate. She'll walk behind us, of course."

"Of course. I was thinking that perhaps we could use each other's Christian names; on account of the engagement we shall soon be announcing. Assuming this conversation goes well, of course," he added, a trifle nervously.

Ava drew in a breath. "I think that is a fine idea, Lord Th – that is, *Dominic*."

He smiled wryly and offered her his arm. "Shall we go in, then?"

She took it, and they stepped into the Park, arm in arm, for the world to see.

*　*　*

Of course, it was hardly *unusual* for a gentleman to walk arm in arm with a lady. In fact, ladies walking alone were generally frowned upon. And it *was* the Fashionable Hour, after all, so most of London Society was gathered in the Park, weather permitting, ready to see who was there and pick up on some gossip, if they could.

They would *note* that Lady Ava Devane was here, walking with Lord Thame, and they would immediately think of that awful scandal sheet article which Ava had steadfastly assured her family that she had forgotten all about.

She hadn't, of course. It wasn't the sort of thing one could forget. Ever.

"I think a key element," Lord Thame – *Dominic* – said slowly, after a moment or two of walking, "is that our union must not be *comical* in the eyes of Society. Mercenary interests are all that is important about a marriage, if Society is to be believed, but heaven help you if you dare say so aloud."

She winced. "I agree. You mean not to make it open that ours is a marriage of convenience?"

"Exactly so. It'll be better that way, I think. No need to convince the world that we're in love, but a little care should be taken, I think."

Yes, we are not *in love,* she reminded herself, with a swallow. It didn't matter what she thought of Lord Thame. Of Dominic. They were friends – acquaintances, really – and that was all.

"Have you told anyone about this?" Ava heard herself say.

"Just one well-trusted friend. What about you?"

"The same. I don't intend to tell my parents. They might see it as their duty to object. They do love me, you see."

He smiled weakly down at her. "They appear to be commendable guardians. Congratulations – not everyone has such a loving family. I do hope they'll like me, at least."

"I'm sure they will. Now, it's rather a basic point, but I had rather make sure. I will have my own rooms in your home, won't I?"

"Of course," he answered hastily. "There is a very fine bedroom with an adjoining dressing-room, washroom, and a large parlour which you can use, or indeed any room that takes your fancy. Downstairs, my wife... that is, she used to use the morning-room as her own personal study. I never set foot in without an invitation. You can use any room that you like, but those rooms in particular will be yours and yours alone. If you have ideas for redecorating the house, or moving things around, please do mention it to me first, although I am not averse to the idea of changing things."

She nodded. "Understand. And what will be expected of me?"

"I want you to take an interest in the children's education. I intend for them all to be well-educated. We have an excellent nurse, who I hope you'll like. You'll have the authority of the children's mother, but she is thoroughly trustworthy. I want the children to like you, Ava. Can you manage that?"

"I think so. I am fond of children, and they generally do like me. All it takes is a little sincerity and interest. I always wanted a family of my own."

"Well, I may be a little biased, but I can assure you that the children are lovely, and very sweet. Daniella is at a... at a difficult age, but you won't be expected to manage her alone."

They rounded a clump of trees, and a great flat field spread out before them, criss-crossed with paths of varying width and smoothness. Carriages rumbled slowly around the edge of the fields. There were plenty of people about, walking in groups of two and three, deep in conversation but simultaneously managing to crane their necks to see what was going on around them.

Ava felt rather exposed.

"I can't think of much else," Dominic said, after a while. "Is there anything else you'd like to know? Once our engagement is official, I think it'll be tricky to break it off. You can, of course, change your mind at any time – I don't want to marry a woman who doesn't wish to marry me – but Society can be unforgiving of that sort of thing."

"I'm aware," she said absently. "I am fully cognizant of the matters with which I shall be grappling, Dominic."

He cleared his throat. The entire affair was quite delicate, reeking of a merchant's arrangement. Ava was not enjoying it, and it wasn't at all like the comfortable, enjoyable conversations she'd had with him earlier.

But then, once this was out of the way, couldn't they go on to be friends, like before? Couldn't they talk and laugh and share plans for the future, just as comfortable as before?

After all, she reminded herself, their marriage would be nothing more than a friendship. Surely that would take the pressure off it all. No silly romance nonsense to think about, nothing but straightforward, practical friendship. Easy.

No reason to feel disappointed. None at all.

She cleared her throat, tossing back her head. "Well, if that's that, I suppose we can turn towards home. I'd like us to discuss this with my parents. I don't much like keeping secrets from them."

"I agree. And Ava..." he trailed off, and she glanced up at him questioningly. His gaze was inward-looking, and he nibbled on his lower lip. "I do mean to make you happy," he said, after a pause. "Marianne was happy with me. I'm a fair man, and a kind one, and you'll have your own money, your own space, and your own comforts. I've said it before, and I'll say it again – I want us to be a team. United."

She swallowed hard. "I want that too. In fact, I must say that..." she paused, a rapid movement catching her eye. Dominic turned to see what – or rather, who – she was looking at, and his face fell, too.

Mrs Ursula Winslow was striding rapidly up the path towards them, a parasol balanced over one shoulder. An elderly maid was puffing and panting along behind her, red-faced and clearly exhausted.

Ava's heart sank. Ursula had a real talent for making a woman feel frumpy and dull, and suddenly it seemed very important that she should not make Ava feel bad in front of Dominic. She glanced up at Dominic and was relieved to find that he simply looked annoyed.

"Lord Thame! Oh, and Lady Ava, too. How nice," Ursula chirped, as soon as she was within earshot. "Oh, Lady Ava, you'll laugh and laugh when you hear what I have to say."

Ava strongly doubted that, but she smiled weakly anyway. "Oh?"

"When I first saw you – I recognised dear Lord Thame at *once*, as he is so very handsome and so *striking* – I quite thought that you were Miss Simmons. You know Miss Simmons, do you not?"

Ava swallowed hard. Miss Simmons was an elderly, unmarried woman in her sixties, known for being rather vulgar, and was kept by her long-suffering brother and his wife. She was a terrible gossip, and generally a person to avoid at parties.

"I don't think Ava looks like Miss Simmons," Dominic said at once.

Ursula glanced up at him, eyes sharpening at the casual use of Ava's Christian name.

"Well, from a distance, you see — it's the gown, I think. That shade of yellow is Miss Simmons' favourite colour, I think, and the old-fashioned style of bonnet. She has the most awful, wiry curls, that eerily resembles the ears of a poodle. One must laugh. But of course, Lady Ava, you are *not* Miss Simmons, although your hair is coming quite out of curl, I must say!"

Ava smiled tightly. There seemed little point in responding to the insult. She felt Dominic's arm tighten around her hand.

"I can't say I see the resemblance myself," he said curtly, in what seemed to be the most uninviting tone he could muster. Ursula didn't take the hint. Standing directly in front of them, she was blocking their path, unless they cared to step around her and walk on the muddy grass. It would be pointed, too, and no doubt Ursula would make something of it.

Behind her, the poor maid caught up, puffing and panting for breath.

"What are you two about, then?" Ursula continued; her tone deceptively sweet. "I heard that you were driving about in the Park only yesterday, and here you are again, walking! I am surprised. Are you so starved for company that you must spend all your time with each other? We must introduce you to some different people, Lord Thame. Don't you think, Lady Ava? Must he not widen his circle?"

Before Ava could respond, Dominic spoke.

"Since you seem to have a little spare time, Mrs Winslow, I have a little information that I think you would like to hear. You'll be the first one to know."

Suspicion crossed her face, although her eyes gleamed at the prospect of hearing something first.

"Oh?"

Dominic glanced down at Ava with a half-smile, and she knew immediately what he was going to say.

"Lady Ava Devane and I are engaged to be married," he announced blandly. "You'll see a notice in *the Gazette* soon enough."

Ursula Winslow blanched, the colour leeching from her face.

Her hands tightened reflexively around the handle of her parasol, and she swallowed thickly.

"Engaged? Well, that *is* a surprise," she managed. "I'm sure that nobody will believe it at first. You two − a couple? Well, stranger things have happened at sea, of course. My congratulations, naturally."

"Thank you," Ava murmured, although Ursula's *congratulations* were almost certainly heavily laced with curses. For a long moment, nobody moved, then at last Ursula seemed to have had enough.

"Well," she said brightly. "I had better go. I'm sure I'll see you both soon."

Goodbyes were murmured, and they stepped aside to let Ursula go past. She strode past, the poor maid groaning and breaking into a light jog again. Ursula did not slow down or glance back, and every line of her body was stiff and tense.

Ava winced. "That has caused quite a stir," she muttered, once they were out of earshot. "That woman hates me. She had her eye on you."

"Don't I know it," he shot back grimly. "I'm not a vain man, and I can't understand what she saw in me."

"Well, now she'll see a challenge. Dominic, you don't think... no, it's ridiculous."

He glanced at her. "What? What were you going to say?"

"Well, I've thought long and hard about who might have given that scandal sheet its information, or even written it for them. Do you think Ursula could have done it?"

Dominic considered for a moment, then shrugged. "She's capable of such a thing, but whether she did or not remains to be seen. We've no proof."

"No, I suppose not. She shall bear a grudge against me, now."

"Yes, but that hardly matters. Once we're married, she can't touch you."

They walked on for a few moments, heading back towards the entrance without needing to discuss it. Ava was heartily sick of walking right about now.

She thought about Ursula, and the odd expression she'd seen flashing across her face, over and over again. It had taken her a while to interpret it, but she'd done it at last.

Jealousy. She had seen jealousy on Ursula Winslow's face.

How odd, Ava thought. *Aside from my engagement to Dominic, why would she be jealous of me?*

And after a moment, another problem presented itself.

More to the point, what does she intend to do about it, and should I be worried?

Chapter Thirteen

"It's not that I don't like the man," Lord Mortensen said, for possibly the hundredth time, "it's just that it's all very *sudden*, you understand? I gave my blessing, of course, and you don't *need* my permission, but..." he trailed off, glancing at his wife for support.

"I'm sure he's a fine man," Lady Mortensen said hesitantly, "but a widower with children... especially one who's enjoyed a fine, happy marriage. You will always be *second best*, darling. You might find yourself compared to his wife – who, being dead, is beyond reproach – more than you would wish. The children might resent you. It's not a fresh start, my dear. If you wish to start your own family..."

"I understand the risks, Mama. Truly, I do. I have it on good authority that his marriage to his previous wife – although happy, was one of convenience."

Lord Mortensen looked sharply at her. "Whose authority?"

She tilted up her chin. "His, as a matter of fact."

They relapsed into silence.

The Mortensen carriage was really only designed to carry four occupants comfortably, or five uncomfortably. Lord and Lady Mortensen sat on one side of the carriage, with Gordon, Ava, and Suzi all crammed into the other side. Beverley and her husband were travelling separately.

The event was a light one, informal, a simple afternoon tea and some light conversation. The purpose of the tea was, of course, to introduce Dominic and his children properly to Ava and her family.

She was nervous. No, nervous seemed too light a word. She felt sick, the carriage jolting her down to her bones, and the whole idea seemed unfathomably ludicrous.

What was she *thinking*? She was engaged now, properly. The notice would appear in *the Gazette* soon, perhaps tomorrow, and now that people knew and her parents had officially given their consent, it was all decided. She was engaged.

"What about your studies, Ava?" Gordon piped up, who'd been remarkably quiet since the news had been broken. "Won't you have to give them up?"

"No," Ava said firmly. "We've talked extensively about the matters. Of course, I'll have the children to manage, but I will also have dedicated parts of the day to myself. There's a perfectly capable housekeeper, so it's not as if I'll have to run the place. There is a nurse and plenty of servants, and Dominic takes good care of his children himself. There's no reason why I can't continue my studies."

"But will he let you?" Gordon prompted. "Some men have odd ideas."

"He will," Ava responded. "I know him well enough to say that."

Gordon seemed satisfied, and Ava felt some of her nerves fizzle away. This wasn't a tempestuous love match, with all sorts of annoying unspoken words passing between them. It had been thoroughly discussed, their schedules arranged, and their respective responsibilities outlined and agreed upon. Ava knew what allowance she would receive every month – she had no idea how she would spend a third of that money, let alone the full amount – and what portion of her day would be hers alone.

Nothing, *nothing* had been left to chance.

She glanced at Suzi, who hadn't said a word since they stepped into the carriage. She'd taken the news of Ava's engagement with mute shock and closed her lips tightly.

"Suzi?" Ava prompted; her voice quiet. "Are you well? You seem preoccupied. This won't detract from your Season, I promise you. We're planning a quiet wedding, but not a *secret* one, to make the gossip columns talk."

Suzi flinched, almost as if a blow had been levelled her way and opened her mouth to speak.

She had no chance to say a word. The carriage began to slow, and Lord Mortensen leaned forward, his eyes bulging with astonishment.

"We're here," he breathed.

***

Dominic hurried through the rooms they'd be using for entertaining – the parlour, followed by the terrace if the weather was fine, and then onto the drawing room – and everything met

93

with his satisfaction.

Mrs Silo, the housekeeper, was a calm and efficient woman, and had run the household since the day Marianne and he had been married.

"All to your liking, your lordship?" the woman asked politely, materializing behind him.

"Yes, very nice, Mrs Silo, thank you."

She hovered for a moment, and he lifted an eyebrow. "Did you wish to ask something?"

"In fact, I did, your lordship." Mrs Silo hesitated, twisting her hands together. "To be frank, I haven't had to manage with a mistress of the house for a long time. Is Lady Ava Devane particular, do you know?"

He smiled wryly. "I think that when she's not helping me care for my children – they'll be *our* children, once we are married – she will be busy with her studies."

"Studies, your lordship?"

"Yes, she has interests in science – natural science, chemistry, mathematics, literature, and so on. She was greatly relieved when I told her about you, and that no real work would be required from her to manage the household. I can wager she won't bother you much."

Mrs Silo blinked, clearly taken aback. "I see. Well, the staff and I look forward to meeting her. May I be so bold as to offer congratulations to your lordship on your engagement? It is a pleasure to all of us to see you so animated, after being alone for so long."

Dominic blinked. *Was* he animated? It was a marriage of convenience, after all. No love involved, even if they *did* like each other. That was what had been agreed, and he would not allow himself to change the goal-posts after the marriage.

"Thank you, Mrs Silo," he managed, after a pause. "You're very kind."

The housekeeper curtsied and went on her way, leaving Dominic free to run upstairs, taking the steps two at a time, and go straight to the nursery.

The house was in order and the food was prepared, but there was something else he was much more worried about.

"What is the special treat this afternoon, Papa?" Steven

94

asked eagerly, allowing Emily to lace up his shoes. "Emily won't tell us."

Emily – who of course knew everything, about the engagement, the marriage of convenience, and so forth – smiled and said nothing.

Maria was playing with her toys in the corner, seemingly disinterested in it all, and Daniella was curled up on her bed, worryingly mulish.

They were all dressed up in their best clothes which, as far as he could tell, was something of a bone of contention.

"Well, some special guests are coming to the house, and they're all very keen to meet you," Dominic said with a smile, crouching down to lace up the other shoe. "There'll be cake, and little pies, and plenty to eat and drink. You can all have as much as you like, so long as you remember your manners as best you can in front of the guests. Everyone is very excited to meet you."

"Can I bring some of my toys?"

"Of course you can, Steven. You all can bring some of your favourite things down to the drawing room. Nurse Emily will help you decide what to bring."

The children immediately grouped together, eagerly discussing which of their favourite things they should bring – which items would intrigue the mysterious guests the most, while providing plenty of amusement for the children should the party get dull."

Smiling to himself, Dominic rose to his feet. The children weren't quite ready, but that was fine. They wouldn't come down until the guests were settled and provided with tea, in any case. He thought he heard the rumble of carriage wheels on the drive and swallowed hard.

It was crucial that this afternoon went well. He shot one last nervous glance at his children, and slipped out of the nursery, closing the door behind him.

***

The party was supposed to be *informal*, but it was anything but. Dominic sat stiffly on the edge of a sofa, with Ava beside him. The others arranged themselves around, glancing awkwardly at each other, waiting for something to break the ice.

I suppose as the host, it's up to me to do that, Dominic thought, and opened his mouth.

"The weather lately has..."

Before he could embark on his truly shocking conversation starter – it wasn't at all like when Ava and he were alone and could easily discuss anything and everything that came to mind, because he had her whole family staring at him, *judging* him – there was a commotion outside and the door banged open.

Maria appeared, beaming, her face smeared with what appeared to be jam.

Dominic rose unsteadily to his feet. "Maria, you..."

Nurse Emily appeared behind her, red-faced and out of breath. "I'm so sorry, your lordships, your ladyships, she ran for it, and I..."

"I was *hungry*," Maria announced.

Steven appeared behind her, looking a little neater but with his laces – now untied, somehow – trailing on the ground.

"I told her to wait," he said, self-importantly. "I told her, Papa."

Nurse Emily attacked Maria's face with a wet washcloth, and a sour-faced Daniella appeared last of all.

"I apologise..." Dominic began unsteady, but Lady Mortensen cut him off with a wave of her hand.

"No apology necessary... we know what it is like to have children. Come on in, little ones, come on in! Who would like a scone with jam and cream?"

Everyone, it seemed.

Lady Beverley Connors seemed to take an immediate liking to Maria, sweeping her up onto her lap and feeding her little meringues.

Steven produced his favourite books and began showing them around, and eventually sat on the sofa beside Ava, who quietly read one of them to him.

Daniella was coaxed out of the hallway, and sat between Gordon and Suzanne, eating a scone and conversing in what she clearly thought was a very grown-up way.

Dominic sank back down onto his seat, feeling a little relieved. He glanced over at Ava, who was hiding a smile.

"See?" she whispered. "Everything is fine. The children are sweet and remarkably well-behaved..."

"Maria came in before she was supposed to, and the jam..."

"Oh, no need to worry. She's a child. Children will be children, Dominic. They're part of the family too, aren't they?"

Dominic smiled at this, the last of his scruples fading away. He stayed quiet, leaning back in his seat to watch the scene. The children were clearly at their ease. Steven abandoned Ava to read books with Lord Mortensen, who affirmed that he could 'do the voices' better than anyone else and had done so for his own children. Maria dragged Suzanne and Gordon into an energetic game of what seemed to be Blind Man's Buff. Hard to tell – and Daniella slipped over to the sofa, sitting between her father and Ava.

"I hear that you are nearly eight, Daniella," Ava said with a smile. "How grown-up you must feel."

That was the right thing to say. Danielle tilted up her chin. "Yes, I am grown-up. Are you a friend of Papa's?"

There was an instant's hesitation. "I am, yes."

Dominic bit the inside of his cheek. He hadn't told the children about the engagement. Perhaps it was a mistake, and perhaps telling them about it now, in front of the guests, was a bad idea, but Daniella was already glancing between them suspiciously.

Get it over with, he told him.

"Children, come here. Maria, Steven, listen to me now." he said, and received the desired attention. He cleared his throat, straightening up a little, and noticed wryly how quiet the room had become.

"As you all know," he said, reciting words he'd lain awake planning out, "Your dear Mamma has been dead and gone for several years now, and we all miss her dearly."

"I miss her most," Daniella piped up. "Since I am older."

Ava took her hand, smiling down at her. "You must tell me all about her sometime. I would love to hear about her."

Daniella brightened. "I can show you some of her old jewels. She would let me play with them sometime, and they are to be mine when I'm old enough."

"How lovely."

"But, it has been a *long time*," Dominic emphasized, "And I have been very lonely. So, I have decided to get married again, and Lady Ava here has decided to marry me."

There was a taut pause while the children thought over these words.

Maria, who was very small and no doubt did not understand the concept at all, shrugged to herself and began playing with a bright blue India-rubber ball she had brought along with her.

Steven frowned, glancing between them.

"But we already have a Mamma," he said, uncertain.

Ava leaned forward. "I know you do. And she won't stop being your Mamma. We'll have her pictures up on the walls, just as they are now, and you can tell me about her, and we'll all remember her together."

This seemed to mollify Steven, but Daniella... oh, dear.

The child was almost shaking with anger. She struggled to her feet, backing away across the sofa.

"You are *not* my Mamma," she shouted, pointing a finger at Ava.

"I know I am not, and I am not trying..."

"I don't want to see you! Go away! Papa, tell her!"

Dominic rose to his feet, seeing Nurse Emily edge towards the child.

"Daniella, we have discussed manners and what is due to guests in our home, and I won't have you speaking to Lady Ava in that manner."

She shook her head, pigtails rasping across her shoulders.

"I hate you," she gasped out. "I hate you, and Mamma hates you too!"

Turning on her heel, she ducked under Emily's outstretched hand and raced out into the hallway, little footsteps fading away.

There was a long, tense silence.

"Well," Lady Mortensen said at last. "Would anyone like any tea?"

Chapter Fourteen

Dominic waited until the others were sitting out on the terrace, laughing and talking and drinking tea. Maria and Steven were behaving themselves – a few mud pies on Maria's side notwithstanding – and seemed entirely at home with their guests.

They both liked Ava, that much was clear to see.

Ava excused herself, getting up from the table and moving inside, no doubt in search of a glass of water. He waited for a moment or two, then followed her.

That is something I like about her, Dominic found himself thinking. *She doesn't make the servants fetch and carry for her all the time. She can take care of herself.*

Not, of course, that it matters, as this is only really a friendship and business arrangement rolled into one, and not *a real marriage.*

"Ava?" he asked, poking his head into the deserted dining room, his eyes slowly adjusting to the gloom.

She was drinking lemonade in the corner, and smiled at him.

"Hello, Dominic. Lemonade?"

"Yes, please. I... I came to apologise."

She lifted an eyebrow, pouring a second glass of lemonade. "Apologise? What for?"

He sighed, edging closer into the room. "For Daniella, of course. I should have warned you. I had an inkling that she wouldn't react well to news of my engagement, and I was right."

Ava nodded thoughtfully, taking a sip of her drink. "Where is she now?"

"The nurse – Emily, by the way, is a remarkably efficient woman, and a part of our family – found her in Marianne's old room. She's been scolded and put to bed. I don't know how you feel about discipline, but I don't strike my children. I don't deprive them of meals, either. Although, perhaps if I took a more conventional approach to disciplining, Daniella would not have made such a scene in the drawing room."

She pursed her lips. "Perhaps. But then her good behaviour would not be based in a firm foundation of good character and strong morals. It would simply be rooted in fear. I don't hold with striking children, either. Or animals, in fact. That's not to say that discipline is an easy thing, but I believe that violence begets more violence, sooner or later."

Dominic released a breath he hadn't even noticed that he was holding. He realized that he was terrified Ava would recommend a strong punishment – bed with supper, and no breakfast in the morning until an apology was given, for example, or perhaps a strapping – and then their ideologies would clash unpleasantly.

"I'm glad. I... I imagine that you think she's spoilt, and perhaps I have overindulged her."

"I don't see a spoilt child. I see a young girl who misses her mother, who worries that her father is going to pull away from her, and she is now afraid that a new Mamma will appear and wipe away all the memories of her mother altogether. So, she is acting in the only way she knows how. At least she gets attention, even though it is the wrong kind."

Ava settled down into one of the chairs, gesturing for him to take the one beside it. He did so, picking up the glass of cool lemonade she'd poured for him.

It was a fine day for the time of year, chilly but not too cold, with warm sunshine to take the edge off the chill and warm the terrace pleasantly. Dominic could hear them talking and laughing out there, Maria and Steven enticing the others to play some game or other.

"I like your children," Ava said suddenly. "They're sweet, and honest, and straightforward. They like people, and love attention, as all children do. I think my family will like them, too. My parents are so excited to greet Beverley's baby, their first grandchild, and that may well be the only grandchild they have for years."

Dominic nodded. "My parents are both dead, and on Marianne's side of the family, only her father remains, so I think the children would like to have grandparents. I think it would be good for them."

"Agreed. As to Daniella, don't worry too much. Give her time to come around the idea of another mother-figure in the house. Something is bothering her about this marriage, and it's up to us to find out what it is. Perhaps it is just that she thinks her mother will be forgotten, but it could be something else."

"Perhaps," he murmured. "I could offer her some sweets, or an increase in her allowance. A pretty dress, perhaps?"

"I think not," Ava said, firm but polite. "Bribery is a bad precedent."

He sighed. "You're right. Please do excuse me. I just... I'm running out of ideas. She was never the sort of child to throw tantrums or declare that she *hated* anybody, but since her mother died, her behaviour has changed."

"Next time I see her," Ava said, half to herself and half to Dominic, "I'll try and talk to her alone. I'll get her to tell me things about her mother, so she knows that I'm not trying to replace her. I'll get to the bottom of this behaviour, if it's the last thing I do. Does she like pretty dresses?"

Dominic nodded. "Very much. Most eight-year-olds do, I'm told."

"Well, perhaps she could be a bridesmaid at the wedding. I'm having Suzi as a bridesmaid, of course, and Willi, and Beverley as the matron of honour, and perhaps if Daniella were included, she would feel better about it all."

Dominic considered this. "Perhaps so. I'll talk to her about it. In the meantime, Ava, I am grateful for what you've done. Your family and you are so good with the children, and I see how Steven and Maria feel at home with you almost at once."

She gave him a quick, surprised smile, as if she hadn't been expecting the praise, then hastily looked away.

Dominic remembered what she'd said about her parents hoping for grandchildren, and how she hadn't mentioned *them* having any children. Because, of course, their marriage would not allow for it. It was a thing of convenience. Besides, would Dominic want to spend time building another family, one which might cause divisions in his own?

Stop it, he scolded himself. *That is not what she wants. Don't put her in an uncomfortable situation. What sort of man are you? Do you not keep to your word, solemnly given? For shame.*

Clearing her throat, Ava rose to her feet.

"If my ears do not deceive me, I think a game is starting out on the terrace. Would you care to join us?"

Dominic smiled, getting to his feet. "I think so."

***

On the way back, Beverley took charge of the seating arrangements in the carriage. The ladies – Beverley herself, Lady Mortensen, Suzi, and of course Ava sat in one carriage, with the gentlemen – Beverley's husband, Lord Mortensen, and Gordon – were set to the second.

It was clear that she had something to discuss.

They climbed into the carriage and waved as they drove away. Ava, who was sitting by the window, watched the figure of Dominic retreat into the distance. He had Maria perched on his shoulders and held Steven's hand. The nurse, Emily – who Ava had had a conversation with, and thought she was a sensible and very likeable woman – stood beside them, calm and collected.

And the drive turned a corner, and they were gone. Ava sat back in her seat with a sigh.

Stop it, Ava told herself firmly. *You knew what this was before you agreed. It doesn't matter how much you like him, or how handsome he is. This is a marriage of convenience. This is a perfectly simple arrangement. Stick to your own part in it, and everything will be fine.*

It didn't matter if her heart plummeted into her stomach every time Dominic looked at her. It didn't matter what she *wanted*, only what they had *agreed*.

It meant that her life would be fulfilled, her status secure, but her studies and her freedom more or less the same. She was lucky. How many other women could say that their lives got *better* after their marriage?

"Well," Beverley said, after a few moments of silence. "What do we all think?"

Lady Mortensen spoke first. "I think the children are sweet. The more I see of Lord Thame, the more I like him. It is clear that he is deeply in love with you, Ava. One can tell by the way he looks at you."

The others nodded, agreeing, and Ava felt a pang of misery. She couldn't possibly explain that it was all a show, to prevent them from looking silly in front of Society. Instead, she smiled weakly and nodded.

"I deemed the eldest daughter to be ill-behaved," Suzi said

vehemently. "I would have given her a sound reprimand, I surmise. Raising her voice so and displaying such heartlessness deserves a forceful response, I believe."

"She's only eight, Suzi," Ava pointed mildly. "She misses her Mamma. Think of how you'd feel if Mama died and Papa brought in a stranger instead."

Suzi's face flushed. "Yes, well. I wouldn't like it, but I wouldn't go on like *that*. She's going to cause you trouble, Ava."

"Ava's right," Lady Mortensen said gently. "She *is* a child, but she can be managed easily, I should think, if you go about it the right way. Harsh punishments are not the way and ignoring her will do no good at all."

"I already talked with Dominic about it. We're going to have her as a bridesmaid."

"Really? How clever of you," Lady Mortensen said, pleasantly surprised.

The three of them began to talk between themselves, and Ava was free to stare out of the window and think.

Beverley was clearly happy with the situation. She was glad that Ava was about to be married, she was properly impressed by Lord Thame, and adored the children.

Suzi, on the other hand, had been behaving strangely, and had been since the engagement was announced. At first, Ava had thought that perhaps it was jealousy, that she was feeling angry that her sister was getting married *now*, at the start of Suzi's first ever Season.

She thought that something else was going on, now, and made a mental note to speak to her sister whenever she had the opportunity. Suzi had warmed up a little bit during the afternoon and had chatted and laughed with Dominic at times.

Everything was going according to plan. It was a good match, everyone said so, and Ava had the pleasure of sitting back and seeing how happy she was making her family. She was marrying a man who was handsome, charming, kind, whose company she thoroughly enjoyed, and who would not stand in the way of her studies and her life.

So why do I feel hollow inside?

She shifted, resting her forehead against the glass of the carriage window and closing her eyes.

103

Don't think about it. Don't allow yourself to think about it.
I love him. I'm falling in love with him.
Too late.

She swallowed hard, opening her eyes and watching the scenery flash by, wishing she could turn her mind and heart off whenever she liked.

Not too long ago, Ava had read a rather interesting novel. The heroine fell in love with the hero early on — or rather, she didn't. Showing a superhuman self-control, she did not *allow* herself to think on him, or to imagine a future with him, until circumstances changed and he made it clear that he was in love with her.

That, of course, happened towards the end of the book. *Belinda*, it was called. She'd enjoyed it, but the heroine had seemed rather... rather *false*. Not quite human.

Perhaps there was a knack to not allowing oneself to feel something, to not dive deep into an emotion that would leave you miserable and unhappy. Perhaps it *could* be done with practice, but either way, Ava did not have the skill for it.

She hadn't even realized she was falling in love with him until it was too late.

How funny, she thought, suppressing a smile. *I'm going to marry the man I love, and yet he's as far out of my reach as if we'd never even met. He doesn't want love. He doesn't love me. He wants a partnership, and I — fool that I am — have just condemned myself to a life of misery. The man I want will be just within my reach, but I will never be able to reach out and have him.*

Well done, Ava, you priceless fool. Well done.

"Ava?"

She jerked upright, her forehead cold and sore from resting against the class. Beverley was watching her curiously.

"Are you alright, my dear? I never asked if *you* had a good time. You are still happy with the match, are you not?"

Ava considered what would happen if she said *no*. There would be a scramble to undo the engagement, to stop the engagement notice reaching *The Gazette*, to stop their friends from finding out. Her family would be frantic, embarrassed, and exhausted. They would do it, of course, if she wished it, but at what cost?

104

Ava smiled back. "Of course I am."

Chapter Fifteen

My Dear Dominic,

Imagine my surprise at reading the notice of your engagement in the Gazette this morning! While I am a little piqued that you did not tell me in person, of course I am thrilled at this news. I sat down immediately to write my congratulations, and here they are.

Lady Ava Devane is, from what I understand, a sensible and respectable young woman. Her portion is not remarkable, and she has a younger sister Out in Society which is generally frowned upon, but that is neither here nor there.

I have not met the lady myself, but I have met her parents, Lord and Lady Mortensen, and found them eminently likeable persons. You have chosen well, I must say, and I extend my congratulations..

Now, as your father-in-law, my permission is naturally not needed. However, let me extend my blessing to you. I would very much like to meet your betrothed, if at all possible. I am assuming that an invitation will be extended to me for the wedding, and I shall offer my acceptance ahead of time.

You and I do not correspond frequently by letter, but I would like to hear how the children are reacting to this change. A new step-mother or step-father can be a tricky business, but they are very small and will, I am sure, get used to the idea quickly.

Regards, and I look forward to your reply,

Lord George Beaumont, the Duke of Mertonshire

PS. I believe that Lady Ava Devane is the sort of woman that my Marianne would have approved of. I wish you all happiness, as I know she would have done.

A lump rose in Dominic throat as he read through his father-in-law's letter. Perhaps he *should* have told the Duke about his engagement ahead of time, instead of letting the man read it in *the Gazette*. It was a little childish, but there was nothing to do about it now.

He sighed, folding up the letter and tossing it back onto his writing desk. He would have to write a reply, and soon. The invitations for the wedding were already going out, and of course the Duke had one, although he wouldn't have received it yet.

Dominic found himself wanting a large wedding. Marianne and he had had a large wedding, and it had been remarkably fun. She'd looked beautiful, he'd enjoyed dressing up in his finest clothes, and they had enjoyed a lovely day of fun, food, and dancing with their friends and family. Some young people saw the wedding as something of inconvenience, to be gotten out of the way with before the marriage could begin in earnest.

Perhaps so, but Dominic had liked all the ceremony and frivolity.

Ava, however, was keen that her wedding should not overshadow her sister's Season in any way. It would be difficult for the wedding not to impact Suzi *at all* – the wedding of a highly eligible widower to a woman who was considered almost an old maid was going to be of interest to Society in general, regardless of how ridiculous it all was.

Dominic kept himself thinking firmly about the logistics of the wedding, rather than the realities of the marriage. It should have made him happy, to think about marrying the woman he was falling in love with.

Shouldn't it?

There was a thump and a muffled yell outside, followed by the cackling of children. Sighing to himself and smothering a smile, Dominic closed up his ledgers and moved out into the hall.

Richard was there, although it was hard to spot him under the pile of children. Dominic leaned in the doorway, arms folded, and watched his friend gradually stagger to his feet. Steven hung from one arm, Daniella from the other, and Maria was clinging onto his back like a monkey, arms tight around his neck.

"I am under attack, my friend," Richard gasped. "Assistance is required at once."

Dominic chuckled, shaking his head. It wasn't often he saw his stern, grim-faced friend crack a little, but the children always seemed to manage that.

One by one, Richard untangled the children from his limbs, and set them rushing off down the hallway, pursued by a hapless maid. He groaned, stretching out his limbs and raking a hand through his ruffled hair.

"They were in fine spirits today," he remarked. "Thanks for the help, by the way."

"I didn't offer any. Care for a splash of brandy?"

"I didn't come here to drink; I came here to find out how the meeting with The Family went along."

Dominic snorted, rolling his eyes. He moved back into the library, and Richard followed, throwing himself into a seat, draping one leg over the arm of the chair.

"Well?" he prompted.

Dominic pursed his lips, thinking how best to tackle this.

"It went smoothly enough," he managed at last. "Everyone was happy, everyone was polite, and I had the impression the family liked me. Ava seemed happy. The children liked them very much, except for Daniella."

"Ah. Now how did I know that Daniella would have been the problem? What happened?"

Dominic told the story, wincing over the memory of his daughter's behaviour. She was in disgrace, that much was clear, and the weight of her father's displeasure and of Nurse Emily's seemed to upset her, but she hadn't yet tried to apologize. Perhaps she would behave better when she met Ava again.

Which was the day after tomorrow, for a trip to Vauxhall Gardens. Vauxhall Gardens had been a renowned and fashionable pleasure garden for many years, and Dominic had been planning to take the children there for a while.

"She's been taking all her meals in the nursery," Dominic said after a pause, "And I told her that her behaviour is unacceptable and that she will have to apologise to Ava."

"And?"

"And she refused."

"Ah," Richard sighed. "She's stubborn. Like you."

"She is not like me."

"She absolutely is. You think she got her stubborn streak from Marianne? No."

This was a point, and Dominic decided not to address it. Instead, he leaned back in his seat and folded his arms tightly over his chest.

"What should I do, then? The marriage is going ahead. Daniella is furious, and I don't know what to do. I haven't known how to handle her for an embarrassingly long time."

Richard pursed his lips, thinking. "Perhaps Ava could have some ideas."

"She does, but how long will her patience last? What if Daniella keeps behaving this way? I'm worrying myself sick about the whole thing, Richard. I want to keep Ava happy, as my wife, but my children are important, too. I'm entirely sure that she's the right choice."

Richard glanced sharply at Dominic at this, his eyes narrowing shrewdly. Dominic felt colour rise to his cheeks, but he forced himself to meet his friend's eye steadily, saying nothing.

"I think she is the right choice, too," Richard said eventually, although as always, Dominic was sure that there was plenty that his friend was keeping back.

Wasn't that always the case with Richard, though?

Before either of them could speak again, there was a tentative tap on the door, and it creaked open.

"Hello, darling," Dominic said smiling despite himself, when Daniella wobbled into the room carrying a small tea-tray, bearing a small teapot, a delicate china cup, and a bowl of sugar. A maid stood behind her, carrying a larger tray with the rest of the things. Mrs Silo stood at the door, watching everything with a benevolent smile.

Beaming, Daniella made her way slowly across the room, setting down the small tray on a coffee-table.

"Miss Daniella wanted to bring in your tea-things, I hope you don't mind. Miss Maria and Master Steven were also keen to help, but I thought it was a bad idea."

"Quite right, quite right, Mrs Silo," Dominic laughed. "Thank you, Daniella. And thank you, Susan, too – you carried the heavier tray!"

The maid smiled and curtsied, backing out of the room

alongside Mrs Silo, leaving Richard and Dominic alone, with Daniella, of course.

Daniella climbed onto her father's lap and leaned back against his chest, nibbling a biscuit.

"I didn't mean to upset you yesterday, Papa," she mumbled at last, and Dominic's heart clenched. He pressed a kiss to the top of her head.

"I know you didn't, darling. But you mustn't talk to Ava like that, do you hear? She would never speak to you in that way. Wasn't she nice and polite to you all the time?"

Daniella wriggled, obviously loathed to admit the truth of this fact. There were a few moments of silence, while the sipped tea and ate biscuits. She grew bored, as eight-year-olds do, and bounced down to bother her Uncle Richard.

He was not, of course, her real uncle, but the children liked to call him that. Dominic was free to sit back and watch his daughter and his closest friend play a game of what seemed to be thumb-wrestling.

"I hear," Richard said, after a few moments of play, "that you are getting a new stepmother, Madam. What do you think of that?"

Daniella pouted. "I don't like it."

"Really? What a shame. Why not?"

Daniella considered this question, and Richard seemed entirely happy to let her mull it over and come to her own conclusion.

"Because, you see," she said at last, "in all the stories, stepmothers are very cruel and evil. It's always an awful thing when the father marries another woman and she is always *terrible*. Besides, I already have a mamma."

Dominic swallowed hard when he overheard this. He saw Richard's eyes narrow, clearly thinking of how he could discuss this matter.

"It is true that you already have a mamma," he said slowly, "but doesn't Lady Ava already know that? I'm sure she doesn't want to take the place of your mamma."

"Perhaps," Daniella acknowledged ungraciously, "But grown-ups often don't say what they mean."

Richard winced. "Well, that is unfortunately true. But Lady

110

Ava, I'm sure, tells the truth. Besides, I know people who sadly lost their mothers, but their stepmothers were just as kind and loving as their real mothers. Perhaps you should give Lady Ava a chance to prove herself."

Daniella didn't seem convinced at all. She suddenly grew bored with the game, and bounced to her feet, glancing back at her father.

"Papa, can I go play in the nursery?"

"Of course you can, my dear. Say goodbye to Uncle Richard."

Daniella did so, offering a wobbly, earnest curtsey that made Dominic smile. She turned and skipped away, humming to herself under her breath.

Dominic's smile faltered when she was gone, and he glanced back to look at Richard.

Richard was not smiling, either.

"She thinks that stepmothers are evil," he murmured. "Of course, all the old fairytales are not particularly complimentary towards second marriages. That'll be a difficult preconception to root out."

Dominic chewed the inside of his cheek. "But surely once she sees that Ava is kind and good, she'll change her mind. They're just stories, after all."

"Sometimes, Dominic, I think you forget that you're dealing with an eight-year-old girl. She's old enough to remember losing her mother, old enough to know what death is and to remember its effects. Her world is changing as she grows, and now, there are greater changes coming, ones that she can't control, no matter how hard she tries. She's only a *child*."

Dominic swallowed past the lump in his throat. "Marianne would have known exactly what to do."

"Perhaps," Richard shrugged. "Perhaps not. The thing is that she is not here, and neither of you would have dealt with a child of Daniella's age in any case. You can only do what seems best to you now. What does Ava say?"

"Ava suggests inviting her to be a bridesmaid. Reminding her that she is part of the family, that sort of thing."

Richard thought this over, nodding slowly. "Ava is a clever woman. Daniella is stubborn, but if you can show her that she is loved, and that her world is not upending the way she thinks it is, she'll settle down. Do you see what I mean?"

Dominic did see, but it didn't change the fact that he had no idea how to manage any of it. What if he made a mistake? Child-rearing was, as the Duke had so kindly pointed out, *difficult*. Yes, it would make a world of difference to know that he was not longer raising his children alone, but it wouldn't change the fact that Ava and he would be outnumbered.

Ava and me. A married couple. Together. United. A partnership. Hard to believe, I think.

Best if he didn't think of it, because then Dominic would have to remind himself that they were living together as friends, not lovers, not a married couple.

Better that than to lose her forever.

He cleared his throat and smiled weakly at Richard. "You're right, of course. Everything will be fine, I'm sure. I'm sure."

Richard eyed him as if he didn't believe him but said nothing.

Chapter Sixteen

Ava had been half-expecting the knock on her bedroom door. She put her book aside and sat up a little straighter.

"Is that you, Suzi? Come in, please."

The door creaked open, and Suzi peered in.

"How did you know it was me?"

"Just a guess. Come, sit down."

Suzi shuffled in, eyeing her warily, and sat down on the low sofa beside Ava.

"You look very pretty today, Ava," she said, in a rush. "Where is it you're going with Lord Thame? It's the Vauxhall Gardens, is it not?"

"That's right. I'm sure the children are getting very excited right about now."

Suzi smiled wanly and said nothing. For a moment or two, there was silence between them. Ava waited patiently for her sister to speak first.

"Beverley gave me a real talking-to last night," Suzi said, after a pause. "She said that this marriage was a good thing for the whole family, but especially for you, and I was wrong not to encourage it. She said I was being thoughtless."

Ava swallowed hard. "I did wonder why she'd dragged you away from the rest of us like that. I wish she hadn't done that."

"She's right, though. I've been quiet about all this, about your marriage. She reprimanded me for my envy, and in that moment, I comprehended. You think I'm jealous, don't you? You think that I worry about my own silly Season, and not thinking about you at all?"

"Suzi, I..."

Suzi whipped around to face her sister, fingers tightening around Ava's wrist.

"I am *not* jealous. If anything, I am worried. I... I know why you're marrying him. You're marrying him because everyone says that you're a simpleton, twenty-six and not married, and that it will reflect badly on me. Well? Is that true? Is that what people have said?"

Ava shifted uncomfortably. "Suzi, it's not so simple. I have reasons for marrying Dominic, and there's a great deal to it. Of course I want your Season to go well, I..."

The hand on her wrist tightened. "Ava," Suzi said, her face vaguely anguished and her voice severe, "Ava, you must not marry this man for my sake. I don't know what your true reasons are, and I daresay they aren't really my business, but do you *promise* me that it's not just for me?"

Ava placed her hand over her sister's, and smiled as reassuringly as she could.

"I promise you, Suzi, I'm not doing this for you. I won't lie, it will be nice not to be a spinster anymore, since Society has decided that unmarried women are *shameful*, and I'll be able to help you so much more during your Season. But I have my reasons for marrying Dominic, and they are good reasons. Don't you want those sweet children to have a good mother? Don't you want to see me happy and settled in Society, as a Marquess' wife, a lady in my own right? I'll have that lovely house, and I'll be able to study as much as I like. I've thought it over and over, Suzi, and this is a good decision."

"But you don't say that you love him," Suzi said flatly.

Ava hesitated, missing a beat.

It would be a lie to say that she did not love him. Things would be easier if she didn't love him, but with every further meeting with Dominic, Ava became more and more resigned to the fact that she *was* in love with him.

Frankly, it was inconvenient.

She opened her mouth, not entirely sure what she was going to say, or even if it was a good idea to speak at all. Unfortunately, whatever Ava was going to say was lost when another tap on the door interrupted them.

"Ava, darling?" Lady Mortensen said, poking her head around the door. "Ah, I thought you'd be in here. Hello, Suzi, darling. Ava, Dominic is here. His carriage is just pulling up outside. Are you ready to go?"

Drawing in a breath, Ava rose to her feet, shaking out her skirts. She held out her arms and did a little twirl.

"Well? What do you think?"

A day out to the Vauxhall Gardens was hardly a trip into high Society, but it was still *Society*, so it was naturally important to look good.

114

Especially when the scandal sheets were so full of her engagement to an eligible widower.

Ava had chosen a maroon-coloured gown, simply cut and plain, and a matching coat, and the ribbon on her bonnet matched, too. Her half-boots were sturdy and suited to plenty of walking.

They would be taking the carriage to their destination, seeing the Vauxhall Gardens, and possibly going for a treat after. The nurse, Emily, would be there, along with a maid to assist, so the outing was perfectly well chaperoned.

And yet, nerves fizzled in Ava's gut like acid. The wedding was going ahead, everything was going well, so why did she worry that something terrible was going to happen?

Lady Mortensen clapped her hands, beaming. "Oh, darling, you look lovely, lovely! Doesn't she, Suzi?"

"Yes, Mama, but Ava always looks lovely."

"Why don't you wear those pretty gold earrings I gave you? Or that emerald set? Oh, yes, Ava, do wear the emeralds!"

Ava shook her head, smoothing out her dress. "We're just going to the Vauxhall Gardens, Mama. No need for emeralds. Besides, I daresay Dominic just wants to see how the two of us can handle the children. I don't need to be dripping with diamonds for that."

Lady Mortensen pursed her lips. "Perhaps, darling, but you must start as you mean to go on. Besides, fond as you are of those children, when you have children of your own, you must consider..."

"I am not going to have children of my own," Ava responded, a little sharper than she should have done.

Her mother blinked, confused, and Ava cursed herself. She shouldn't have said that.

"What? Whyever not? I know that some couples are unlucky and simply are *not* blessed with children, but that's not to say..." her voice faded away, uncomfortable.

Ava cleared her throat, wishing she'd been more careful. There was no need to let on that there was no love in this marriage.

Not on Dominic's side, in any case.

Glancing out of her window, she saw Dominic's carriage drawing up in front of the steps.

"I must go, Mama. He's here."

She hurried out without waiting for a reply.

***

The children were positively simmering with excitement.

That is, Steven and Maria were. Daniella sat opposite Ava on the other side of the carriage, eyeing her mulishly, arms folded.

Dominic sat beside Ava, and she found herself wishing they had chosen different seats. Not that he was leaning close to her, but still.

"I want to see the firework displays," Steven said stoutly. "Can we go straight to see them, Lady Ava?"

"Of course," Ava said with a laugh. "And you don't need to call me *Lady* Ava."

"You mustn't call her Mamma, because she is *not* our Mamma," Daniella interjected sullenly.

Dominic frowned, and leaned forward to scold her. Ava laid a hand on his arm.

"Daniella is right, children, I am *not* your Mamma. I am going to love you as if I *were* your Mamma, and I hope that you will love me, but we shan't forget your real Mamma, not ever." She said, smiling at all three of them. Daniella did not smile back, but Ava smiled at her anyway.

"Mama's favourite colour was blue," Steven offered.

"How lovely! Perhaps once a year, on the day that would have been her birthday, we could do something to celebrate, and we could all wear blue? Would you like that?"

Daniella scowled harder. "You don't mean that."

"Daniella," Dominic said, warningly. "You promised to behave."

Ava smiled at him. "I'm sure Daniella will feel a little more comfortable once we get there. I daresay she's all cramped up in this carriage – I know I am!"

The children – not Daniella – chatted on until they reached their destination, and they tumbled out and into the wide, paved walkways of the Vauxhall Gardens.

There was so much to see, and so little time. All three of the

116

children wanted to go in different directions – Daniella wanted to explore the beautiful gardens, while Steven was excited to see the fireworks. Maria, on the other hand, was intrigued by the majestic peacocks, even though she struggled to pronounce their name correctly.

"One at a time, one at a time!" Dominic said, laughing and unfolding a paper map of the gardens. "Now, this map shows me where everything is, so we shall go through it in an orderly fashion and see everything, instead of all three of you pulling me in different directions."

Perhaps it was the lengthy carriage ride or simply a bad mood, but Ava was horrified to see tears start into Daniella's eyes.

"But I *want* to see the beautiful landscaped gardens, Papa!" she insisted.

Ava glanced around. Judging by the surprise on Nurse Emily's face, this sort of tantrum was not usual for Daniella. Dominic, however, scowled.

"Don't be silly, Daniella. You will see the gardens, but first…"

She stamped her little foot. "I *want* to see the gardens, and I am not a silly girl! I am not, I am not!"

Dominic's expression darkened. "I have had quite enough of this. Daniella, you are going back to the carriage. If you can't be trusted to behave, then you won't have a treat. Emily, would you take her?" He reached for Daniella, who gave a squawk of panic and dodged away.

"Dominic, may I?" Ava said quietly. Dominic blinked at her, a little surprised, but nodded wordlessly.

She moved over to Daniella, kneeling down before her, and took her hands in hers. Ordinarily, the child would likely not have allowed it, but at the moment she was so tearful and hysterical she just stood there, motionless.

"Daniella," Ava said firmly. "I know this is not like you, to make such a fuss. Your Papa has promised that you will see the gardens, just like Maria will see her peacocks and Steven the fireworks. I know you're a kind girl, and very loving towards your brother and sister. So, it would be nice to arrange our journey so they can see what they want as it is in our way first, don't you think?"

Daniella sniffled, seeming subdued. "I didn't mean to be

unkind."

"I know you didn't. But you're getting older now, and that means you have to stay calm even when something upsets you. When my little sister was your age, she sometimes got very upset and angry about things, and wouldn't listen to reason. I did it too. Now, I know you're a clever, sensible, *fair* girl. This is a treat for everyone, and I'm sure you won't want to ruin it − or spend the rest of the afternoon in the carriage."

"I don't want to go back to the carriage."

"And you won't, so long as you behave. I know you *can* behave, Daniella."

She sniffled again, wiping the back of her nose with her hand. The girl seemed to come to herself, pulling her other hand out of Ava's, and turned to her father.

"I'm sorry, Papa," she said quietly. "I just wanted to see the gardens."

He bent down and kissed the top of her head. "And you will, just be patient, yes?"

She nodded, and he pinched her cheek.

"That's my good girl. Now, to celebrate our getting here, shall we have a piece of apple tart each?"

This was met with squeals of delight, and Ava had to suppress a smile. Dominic glanced at her and lifted his eyebrows.

"We *all* have treats on outings, Nurse Emily and her assistants included. Can I assume you'll have a piece, Ava?"

She grinned, looping one arm through his.

"You assume correctly."

They made their way across the crowded courtyard towards a stall selling a variety of desserts with apples, the children already pointing out the piece which caught their fancy.

Ava found herself glancing up at Dominic, who was smiling fondly at his children, shaking his head. Her chest clenched, her heart feeling as if it were being squeezed inside a giant fist.

Oh dear, she thought bleakly. *This is not good for me. Oh, dear.*

Chapter Seventeen

The trip to the Vauxhall Gardens had not been, in Dominic's opinion, an *absolute* disaster.

Part of him wanted to quit while he was ahead and go immediately home, but he had promised the children a treat afterwards, and a treat they must have.

"We'll go to Gunters for ices," he promised, sweeping Maria up into his arms. The children gave squeals of delight, already planning what flavour ice they would get, and in what shape. At the moment, the fashion was for most impressively moulded ices and sorbets, designed to look like anything but ice. The fashion was also to walk around the square or go back to their carriages with the ices, but Dominic had already decided that they would eat inside the shop. It would be easier to manage the children and eat their own ices then.

They entered the shop, a genteelly tinkling bell heralding their arrival, and the children hurried forward to see the shaped ices on the waiters' trays. Dominic and Ava fell behind a little, arm in arm, as was proper for a gentleman escorting a lady.

"Thank you for what you did earlier," Dominic said quietly. "With Daniella, I mean. I sometimes don't know how to manage her at all, and I just know that I can't allow her behaviour to continue."

She nodded. "It's nothing, really. I think Daniella is hurting. It's a tricky age, and I believe she has a sense that her whole life is upending, and that she has no way of keeping it even. She's frightened, you know."

A lump rose to Dominic's throat.

"I remember holding her in my arms only an hour after she was born. She was so small and fragile. She didn't cry, only looked up at me with large eyes. She seemed curious, and I felt... well, it was a difficult sensation to put into words. Everything, all at once."

He glanced down at Ava, wondering if she wasn't enjoying his talk about his family. To his surprise, her expression was pensive, and fixed firmly on him.

"We'll manage," she assured him quietly. "Together."

Dominic's heart swelled. He'd picked the right woman, he

knew it. With Ava at his side, the perils of raising children didn't seem quite so terrifying. And he'd have a wife once again, a partner.

But not a lover, a snide voice in his head warned. *You might as well be marrying Nurse Emily for all the feelings Ava has for you.*

Then they had reached the counter, and there was no time to indulge in such miserable thoughts. It was time to order their ices, and the children were tugging eagerly on the tails of his jacket, clamouring for the ice of choice.

The children wanted ices shaped like fruit — Daniella choosing an apple-shaped ice, Steven a pear-shaped one, and Maria an ice shaped like a bunch of grapes. Ava chose a chocolate ice in a more ordinary shape, and Dominic a brown bread ice.

They retreated to a table to wait for their orders, and the children eagerly talked about the Vauxhall Gardens and about everything that had made an impression on them.

"I think it is a shame," Daniella said stoutly. "For people to be confined within the walls of Vauxhall Gardens in order to enjoy the natural beauty."

"That is a very clever thought, Daniella," Ava commended her.

Daniella initially beamed at the praise, then seemed to remember that Ava was the one giving it to her and scowled instead. Ava pretended not to notice.

Their ices arrived, and they ate in comfortable silence for a moment or two.

After a while, Ava cleared her throat, gently setting down her spoon.

"Children, I was wondering if I could talk to you about something. As you know, your Papa and I are getting married. We're getting married soon, in fact, and the wedding is going to be a fine one. I have spoken to your father about this, and he is happy to agree, but I need to ask your permission, too. I was hoping that you would all be a part of my bridal party."

"Bridal party?" Steven queried, wrinkling his nose.

"Yes, I was hoping that Daniella would be a bridesmaid with my sisters and my dearest friend. Maria can be a flower girl, and you, Steven, could be a page boy, and perhaps help your Papa hold the rings and such. What do you say?"

"Will I have to wear a dress?" Steven asked, in a hushed tone of horror, and Ava chuckled.

"Not unless you want to."

This seemed to relieve him, and he sat back in his seat, considering.

"I would like it very much," he said at last, and Maria nodded eagerly. She had ice cream smeared all around her mouth, and poor Nurse Emily in the next booth was clearly itching to wipe it away, being almost distracted from her own ice.

Dominic and Ava glanced at Daniella at the same time, eyebrows lifting hopefully.

It was silly to hope that his oldest daughter had entirely changed her character in the space it had taken her to eat one ice. She had her arms folded, lips pressed together mulishly, and looked nothing short of furious.

"I don't want to be your bridesmaid," she said stoutly. "I won't do it, and you can't make me!"

Colour rushed to Dominic's face. Daniella had raised her voice, and although there were only a few customers in the shop, most of them glanced narrowly at the family, eyebrows raised in judgement. He leaned forward across the table, dropping his voice.

"Daniella, I am not going to sit here and listen to you..." he trailed off when Ava laid her hand delicately on his forearm. Her hand rested on his sleeve, but the tips of her fingers brushed the back of his hand. It was an accident, of course it was, but that didn't stop shivers running along his skin, the points of contact prickling with heat.

"It's quite alright, Dominic," she said calmly, and smiled wryly at Daniella. "That is disappointing, Daniella. But I asked your permission, and you have said no. Nobody is going to make you do anything you feel so strongly about. You aren't *obliged* to join my bridal party, and I wouldn't dream of making you."

Daniella, who had almost certainly expected more of an argument, blinked around in confusion, glancing at her father as if for explanation.

It was not forthcoming. Dominic took a few deep breaths – he had a temper, he knew, and it simply wouldn't do to display that temper in front of his impressionable children – and flashed a quick smile at his daughter.

121

They began eating again, although Daniella still looked confused.

"What will I wear?" Steven piped up, glancing around the table.

"I'm glad you asked," Ava said, laughing. "We have the outfits all picked out. I will be wearing a pale blue dress, with the loveliest lace, and Maria will have a little gown to match. You, Steven, are going to wear a dark-blue suit like your Papa. It's all silk and satin, with an old-fashioned cravat which is all lace and the finest muslin. It seems a lot of work to put into one day, but weddings only come once in a lifetime, after all. Besides, your Papa is an important man, and lots of people will be coming to the wedding."

"What does a flower girl do?" Maria asked, licking her spoon.

"You'll go ahead of me with a basket of flower petals and scatter them all over the aisle. You shall have a little basket with a long handle and a blue ribbon around the edge. How does that sound?"

Maria considered this seriously for a moment. "It sounds very grand." She said at last.

Dominic, whose participation in his own wedding had been fairly limited until now, was able to sit back and finish his ice, listening to the conversation go along without him. Ava chatted easily to the children, trying and failing occasionally to draw Daniella into the conversation.

Daniella looked more and more unhappy by the minute. She had finished her ice and pushed away the plate, sitting with her arms folded and her lip pushed out, for all the world as if she were half her age instead. When Ava started talking about the fabric they had bought for the bridesmaid's dress, he thought that she might actually cry.

"Daniella?" Dominic asked quietly, leaning forward over the table. "You look upset. Did you not like your ice?"

He knew fine well what the problem was, and it had nothing to do with her ice. Daniella was feeling left out. Her pride had made her refuse the offer to be bridesmaid, a position which was sounding more fun by the minute. Especially since her brother and sister were going to be part of the bridal party.

"My ice was very nice, Papa," Daniella muttered. "Thank

you."

Dominic nodded, swirling his spoon in the half-melted dregs of his ice.

"It's such a pity you don't want to be Ava's bridesmaid. It sounds like a great deal of fun, don't you think?"

This comment had the desired effect. Daniella sank further down in her chair, looking miserable.

Sharp as always, Ava glanced their way, taking in the situation in an instant.

"Yes, it is a shame," she said calmly. "The material for the bridesmaid dresses is already ordered, and I daresay there'll be a surplus."

Daniella shifted in her seat again, nibbling her lower lip.

"Well, if you've already ordered the material," she said brusquely, "I don't want to be troublesome."

It was hardly a gracious acceptance. Dominic winced, glancing over at Ava. He wouldn't have blamed her for bristling at this. Instead, Ava was smiling.

"So, you'll be a bridesmaid, then?"

She waited for a response, which was a long time coming."

"Yes, I will be a bridesmaid," Daniella mumbled at last, and a beam spread over Ava's face.

"Well, isn't that lovely news! I'm very glad you changed your mind, Daniella."

"It's only so that the material doesn't go to waste," Daniella insisted lamely, probably aware that she wasn't fooling anyone.

"Of course," Ava said smoothly, still smiling. "Now, let's talk about what your dress will look like. Given that we are fashioning the gowns entirely anew, you and Maria can have different styles of dress. What do you think?"

Dominic sat back in his seat again, letting the conversation go by without him. Ava spoke just as easily to the children as she did to adults, and it was clear that Steven and Maria were already warming to her. Daniella was resisting, of course – nothing that girl did was ever easy – but the subject of dresses and colours and styles was already something she was interested in.

Strange how the children are so different, he thought wryly. *Daniella is a classic little girl, who likes gowns and pretty things. Steven is a scholar who already likes to avoid people, and if Maria's propensity for making mud pies and then attempting to eat them signifies anything, she'll grow up to be a tomboy. Wonderful.*

At last, the conversation came to an end and the sun shifted in the sky, and Dominic reluctantly announced that it was time to go home.

Outside, the streets of London were emptying, with ladies and gentlemen going home to dress and refresh themselves before the night's entertainment began – parties and balls and soirees, or any number of fashionable events.

They dropped Ava off at her home, and the carriage rumbled on home.

"I like Ava," Steven announced drowsily, curled up against his father's side. Maria was already fast asleep, sitting on her father's lap and leaning against his chest. Daniella sat on Dominic's other side, arm looped through his, cheek resting against his shoulder.

She said nothing.

"I like Ava too," Dominic said quietly. "I think she'll make a good mamma to you all."

"We already have a mamma," Daniella said instantly. Dominic slid an arm around her shoulder, squeezing her tight.

"I know that, darling," he murmured. "And Ava knows it, too. You mustn't worry about that."

Daniella's lip pushed out again. It was a habit she'd had when she was younger, and it resurfaced when she was tired. Dominic recalled a brief memory of his wife crouching down before their petulant daughter, laughing and coaxing her out of her bad humour.

It wasn't a skill he had ever possessed. Surely their daughter deserved better.

"Ava likes you all very much," Dominic found himself saying. "She wants to make you all happy, she wants us to be a family. I think your mamma would have liked her, too."

Daniella looked as though she wanted to disagree.

Chapter Eighteen

"I think I'm making progress with her. I really do," Ava murmured, keeping her voice low-pitched so that neither the modiste nor the little girl staring at the ribbons could overhear her.

Suzi glanced over her shoulder, glancing at Daniella, and pursed her lips.

"I hope so, Ava, for your sake."

The material for the bridesmaid dresses might be brought, but there was a great deal left to get – buttons, lace, beads, trimmings, and a tremendous quantity of thread, to say nothing of the hanks of embroidery thread that Lady Mortensen thought necessary.

So, they had visited Madame Peu's, a talented modiste who was certainly not French, regardless of the accent she affected, and were stocking up on the materials they would need.

The wedding, as Ava remembered frequently, was creeping closer and closer, unstoppably so.

She wasn't sure if she should feel pleased or aghast. This wedding was what she wanted, after all. Something logical, well-ordered, based entirely on matching principles and goals. And... and it wasn't as if she didn't feel *affection* for Dominic. Perhaps too much, really. Their marriage was going to be a sensible one, and she ought to keep her feelings in check. She had better, or else she would find herself in quite a predicament.

Romance was really not the thing these days. Novels and giddy young women might *claim* to value love and romance above all things, but in the real world, marriage was a much more mercenary matter.

I am doing the right thing, Ava told herself severely. *This is the best thing for me. It will suit everybody. If I can just win over the children – Daniella, really – then all will be well.*

Maria and Steven were really too small for a modiste's shop, but Daniella seemed eager to come. The other two children, along with Dominic, would meet them back at Ava's home, for a light luncheon.

Ava had paid a quick visit to the toy shop before they came here and had a present for each of the children tucked away in a box. She'd spent far too long agonising over her choices, as if her future depended on how much the three children liked their toys.

She moved away from the modiste – who was none too subtly trying to distract Suzi's attention from the cheap beads to the expensive ones and was currently expounding the benefits of sequins – and headed towards Daniella.

"They're pretty, aren't they?" Ava said with a smile, reaching out and running her fingers over the rows of brightly coloured ribbons.

"Papa says I have enough ribbons," Daniella said mournfully. "My favourites are the yellow ribbons that Grandpapa gave me as a present."

"Shops like this are all set up to tempt us into buying more than we need," Ava explained, keeping her voice low in case the modiste took offence. "There's nothing wrong with having pretty things, not at all, but there are many people in the world who have to make do with string instead of ribbon, and who can't even afford food, let alone pretty things."

Daniella considered this. "When I am grown, I am going to make sure that everybody is taken care of."

"Everybody? Goodness, what large plans," Ava said, laughing.

"I can do it, I'm sure!"

"I'm sure you can do whatever you put your mind to, my dear. Now, come and take a look at this brocaded material we can use for sleeves, and tell me what you think."

Daniella brightened up, and Ava silently congratulated herself. She was doing well, she thought. So far, so good.

"I had a doll with a brocade dress when I was little," Daniella confided, as they made their way across the room. "Mama made the dress for me. She was very good at making dresses. It was my favourite."

"Oh, how lovely! What was the doll's name?"

"Amy. But she broke, a year ago. It was an accident. I dropped her, and her head – which was made of china – shattered. Papa tried to stick her together again, but it wouldn't work."

Daniella wilted a little, and Ava bit her lip. She could imagine how a child of her age would treasure a doll, especially one that was gifted from her beloved late mother, dressed in a gown of her mother's making.

Her own gift to Daniella seemed even more fortuitous now, but that would have to wait.

"Well, I'm sorry for it," Ava said at last. "But I hope you kept the dress?"

Daniella nodded. "I did, but it doesn't fit any of my other dolls."

Then they had reached the modiste's counter, where various coloured of brocaded fabric were spread out for their perusal, and Daniella seemed to forget all about dolls.

***

"... and you should have seen all the colours, Papa!" Daniella chirped. "Every colour you could *possibly* imagine, and *more!*"

Dominic laughed, taking a sip of his tea. "It sounds like you've had a fine outing."

His gaze slipped past his daughter and landed on Ava. She hadn't been expecting him to look at her right then, and a shiver rolled down her spine. Clearing her throat, Ava took a large sip of her own tea – which was too hot and burned her tongue – and tried to remind herself that this luncheon was all about the children, not about Dominic and her.

There *was* no *Dominic and her*, anyway. Clearing her throat, she flashed a quick, cool smile at Dominic, and his gaze slid away, back to Daniella, who was chattering away about what she'd seen and tried on at the modiste's.

"It sounds like you are quite looking forward to the wedding, then?" Dominic said, when the babble had drawn to a halt.

Daniella flushed. "I'm not, *not* looking forward to it."

He nodded seriously, as if this made sense.

They had gone back to Beverley's house, where the engagement party had been thrown only a few days ago.

Really, the party had been unremarkable. The infatuation was exceedingly intense – Beverley had apparently decided to invite the whole of London – that Ava had barely seen her own betrothed.

It shouldn't have bothered her as much as it did. Dominic wasn't *hers*, after all.

And wretched Ursula Winslow had been there, and cornered Ava. She'd been so thoroughly unpleasant and sly that Ava had been hard pressed not to throw her entire glass of champagne on the woman. It had been tempting, too – the scandal sheets would have plenty to say about it, but she *could* pass it off as an accident.

But she had kept a firm grip on her drink, and smiled fixedly until Beverley finally noticed that something was wrong and came to rescue her. Ava was more certain than ever that Ursula had been the one to speak to the scandal sheets about her. Naturally, it could not be proved, and even if it could, all it would do was dent the woman's already tenuous reputation.

I am engaged to Dominic, Ava thought furiously. *Not her.*

She gave herself a little shake, coming back to the present. Her parents were in the corner, conversing in low tones, and Suzi was kneeling on the floor, playing with Maria.

It's time for the presents, Ava thought, with an unusual surge of nerves. She caught Beverley's eye, who slid the boxes out from behind the sofa.

Daniella noticed at once, sitting up a little straighter and frowning.

"Since you three have been so kind and well-behaved today, and have so nicely agreed to be part of my wedding," Ava said, "I bought you all a little gift. Maria, the pink box is for you, the green one is for Steven, and the rectangular blue box is for Daniella."

The children gave squeals of delight, darting towards their presents.

"What do you say, children?" Dominic chipped in, laughing.

They chorused their thank-yous, and Maria got up to kiss Ava on the cheek.

"Don't thank me yet," she said, laughing. "You haven't seen your presents yet."

Maria excitedly tore off the wrapping on her pink present, revealing a new, stuffed rabbit toy, its soft fur striped in blue and pink, its eyes a shiny black. It was a long toy, almost as long as Maria when she lifted it up, squealing with delight.

She hugged the toy ferociously and rushed over to kiss Ava again.

"Thank you, Ava," she said, beaming. "I shall call her Alice."

"That is an excellent name for a rabbit," Dominic said,

laughing. His eyes met Ava's, and there was something in them that she couldn't read. But there was no time to think about it, because then Steven took the lid of his box to reveal a set of cunningly carved and neatly painted wooden animals.

He sucked in a breath, his face going red with pleasure. He took out the camel, painted a sandy brown with black eyes and a tiny, multicoloured blanket affixed to its hump.

"Thank you, Ava," he said, echoing his sister, more quietly. She gave him a nod.

"I know how you love animals, Steven. I hope you don't already have a set like this?"

He shook his head, taking the animals out one by one and carefully inspecting them.

Then it was Daniella's turn. Ava felt a fistful of nerves clench in her stomach.

Gingerly, Daniella removed the lid, to reveal a doll about the length of a person's forearm, from elbow to fingertips.

Ava had agonized over the choice of doll. There were so many to choose from in the shop, with different faces, different clothes, different colours. This doll had a smooth wooden body, with moveable limbs, and china for its head, neck, hands, and feet. It had smooth black hair, large blue eyes that opened and closed, and a blue brocaded dress and slippers to match.

She hadn't meant to choose brocade, it only seemed right because there would be blue brocade on the bridesmaid's dress. Now, remembering the story Daniella had told her about her mother's doll, it seemed perfect.

Ava realised that she was holding her breath. She glanced up at Dominic, and found him watching Daniella, expectant.

The little girl's face flitted over the doll, emotions warring on her face. She fingered the brocade, and tears glittered in her eyes.

Without warning, she threw the doll back in the box and sat back, arms crossed tightly over her chest.

"I don't like it," she announced stoutly. "It's ugly."

There was a general intake of breath. Steven ducked his head, and Maria hugged Rabbit Alice close to her chest.

"Daniella!" Dominic barked out. "Where are your manners? That is a beautiful doll."

Daniella shook her head hard, curls flying out around her

face.

"She only bought it because I told her about Mama's doll!" She shouted accusingly, pointing a finger at Ava. "Mama's doll and the brocade dress. I don't need your silly doll. I don't *need* it!"

"Daniella, dear, it was just a coincidence," Ava tried. "The dress was just meant to match your bridesmaid's gown."

"I don't believe you," Daniella snapped.

There was a stunned silence in the room. Lord and Lady Mortensen were pretending not to have noticed, Beverley seemed to be on the brink of tears, and Suzi was glaring at the girl.

Dominic had gone crimson.

"Ava is not trying to upset you," he said sharply, and Ava saw that he was really angry now. "It was a lovely gift, and here you are being so awfully rude about it. I'm ashamed of you. Say that you're sorry, right now."

His tone was wrong, his words too angry. It wasn't going to work. Ava saw tears glitter on Daniella's cheeks, before she ducked her head to hide them. She turned away, refusing to even look at the doll.

"I hate her," she said bitterly. "I hate her and I hate the doll."

Dominic leapt to his feet. "I have had quite enough of you, young lady. Emily, take her back to the carriage immediately. You are in deep trouble, Daniella. You have gone too far, and you can expect to be seriously punished when we get home."

Daniella pressed her lips together, jutting out her chin. She got to her feet when the nurse came hurrying over, face pale and shocked.

The atmosphere in the room was stiff and tense, the joy of the day gone altogether. Dominic was still on his feet, red-faced, as Daniella was hustled out of the room, the nurse gripping her arm tightly.

"Steven, Maria, pack up your toys," Dominic said, after a taut pause. "Steven, pack up Daniella's doll, too. Ava, I... I cannot apologise enough. I don't know what's gotten into her, especially after you were so kind."

"It was poor timing," Ava said with a sigh, rising to her feet. It felt like the day was ruined. Well, perhaps it was. "She told me about a doll her mother gave her, with a brocade dress, and I suppose she felt as if I were trying to replace the doll and the

130

dress."

"She'll be punished, Ava, I promise you."

Ava bit her lip. "She's just a child."

Dominic took his leave quickly after that, as if embarrassed. Well, he probably was. The maids came in to clear the tea-things, and the family sat around, stiff and silent.

Ava sat in her seat, hardly aware of what was going on around her.

We have returned to the initial point, she thought bitterly. *It's as if all the progress I made with the girl is undone, just like that.*

Suzi came to sit beside her.

"Are you well?" she asked quietly.

Ava nodded, hesitated, then shook her head.

"I don't know what to do, Suzi. I just don't know what to do next."

Suzi took her hand and said nothing. There really wasn't anything *to* say.

Chapter Nineteen

All of Society is talking about the wedding of the Season, between eligible widower Lord Dominic Broughton, Marquess of Thame, and infamous spinster – at the advanced age of twenty-six – Lady Ava Devane. Readers may recall that these two people have already appeared within the pages of this column, with the renowned spinster said to be ardently pursuing the still grief-stricken widower.

While Lady Ava's actions have been thoroughly censured by Society, by various persons urging her to leave the youthful 30-year-old Marquess to younger or at least richer women, it seems that the wedding is to go ahead after all.

Invitations have been received, and a wedding breakfast is to be held at the Mortensen home, with the Marquess' children in attendance. Anyone could be there, with their own opinions to boot.

Are we looking at the most devastatingly ill-matched marriage of the year? Will this hasty match bring anything beyond misery and regret? Or, perhaps, are we about to see the love-match of the century?

This author thinks not. Despite their apparent devotion to each other – and to the Marquess' children – this author has it on good authority that the match is a coldly mercenary one, with money and a good establishment the primary concern over the melding of hearts.

This author must echo their earlier sentiments towards this whole business – for shame, Lady A, for shame!

Let us hope that the dear Marquess does not find himself repenting in his leisure what he enacted in his haste. However, regardless of the fate of this match, let us all gather to watch the wedding take place tomorrow – place your bets, ladies and gentlemen, place your bets!

"You were mentioned in the gossip columns this morning," Suzi observed.

Ava, sitting before her looking-glass while the maid diligently twisted her curls on top of her head, sighed deeply.

"I don't care, Suzi."

"I just… just thought you'd want to know."

Ava said nothing. She'd guessed that she would be mentioned. The scandal sheets were thrilled at the news of the engagement between Dominic and Ava, since it had been classed such a poor match. It seemed that Dominic, at the age of thirty, was solidly in his prime, if not still in his youth, but at twenty-six, Ava was a dried-up old maid that nobody would ever want. Apparently, it was just as ridiculous for him to marry her as it would be for him to marry some fifty-year-old dowager.

It was all nonsense, of course, but reading it over and over again in black-and-white tended to take its toll after a while. It was hurtful to know that so many people thought of her that way. Yes, perhaps the people who *truly* mattered didn't think that way, but it still *hurt*.

Whoever said that *sticks and stones may break my bones but words will never hurt me* had clearly never read article after article describing her as a dull, dried up old maid who was out to 'catch' a man and make his life miserable.

Ugh.

"Done, milady," the maid said, stepping back. "You look beautiful, madam, if I may be so bold."

Ava smiled faintly at the woman.

She *did* look beautiful. Her thick hair was curled well and piled up on top of her head, secured with blue glass flowers, sparkling in the depths of her hair like jewels.

Her gown was heavier than she'd expected, and much finer and more ornate than what she was used to. The sleeves were trimmed with the brocade fabric, matching the bridesmaids' gown.

She rose, watching the fabric spill down to pool around her feet.

I don't feel like me, she thought numbly. The beautiful woman in unimaginable finery that greeted her in the mirror was *not* Ava Devane, bluestocking and intellectual. She was…

Well, she was a bride.

She drew in a deep, shuddering breath. "Beverley? Can I talk to you privately, please?"

This earned her a few curious stares, but Beverley made an impatient gesture, and the others scuttled out. Suzi went too, albeit reluctantly. The door closed softly behind them.

"Alright," Beverley said sternly. "Are you going to tell me what's going on?"

"I'm just… just nervous, I suppose. Am I doing the right thing, Beverley?"

Beverley did not immediately respond. She circled Ava, apparently eyeing her dress, making adjustments here and there. She smoothed the lace collar and tweaked the brocade sleeves, adjusting the set of the sapphires around Ava's neck.

"Lord Thame is a good man," she said finally. "Do you disagree?"

"No, of course not."

"Despite his insufferable oldest daughter, he's a fine man, with plenty to offer. You'll have a proper establishment, you'll have status in the world, as well as wealth and a ready-made family. You heard all those awful things the scandal sheets said about you. Or read them, rather. It's so cruel, but the world *is* cruel to women. If you stay unmarried for much longer, they'll be even more cruel."

Ava bit her lip, tilting up her chin. "I'm not marrying to escape censure."

"No, but you *do* have your reasons, don't you?" Beverley prodded gently. "Marriage is seldom prompted by only one aim. It's a number of reasons, and not least of all is the affection and esteem you hold for the other person. And you *do* esteem Lord Thame, do you?"

Ava flushed. She could see her cheeks turning pink in the mirror. It felt like an understatement to say that she esteemed him.

I do believe I am falling in love with him. Which is not ideal, since love has nothing to do with our respective reasons for marriage.

"Of course," she heard herself say. Beverley eyed her for a long moment, and Ava had the unpleasant feeling that her sister understood more than Ava had intended her to understand.

"Good," she said at last. "Well, since this marriage is a good thing for you both – and it *is* a good thing for you both – and calling it off now would ruin your reputation beyond repair, to say nothing of humiliating Lord Thame and his family, I think perhaps we should think of leaving for the church, don't you think?"

Ava swallowed, nodding. "You're right. Thank you, Beverley.

134

I appreciate you sensible good sense at times like this."

"Since you are usually the one who provides said sensible *good sense*, it is certainly my turn. Now, do you have everything?"

"Yes, I do."

A modest bunch of flowers, tied with a pale blue satin ribbon, lay on the dressing-table, made up of wildflowers, grasses, and greenery. It was more simple than was fashionable – large hot-house flowers and a profusion of roses were the preferred flowers of the Fashionable Set at the moment – but Ava liked them and intended to keep them. She would press them between the pages of books and keep them forever.

Beverley gave her one last inspection, circling her again and tweaking at the falls of fabric, then nodded firmly.

"Time to go," she said, her voice softer than it had been before. "My little sister, getting married at last. I can scarcely believe it."

Ava smiled weakly. "And neither can I."

***

The wedding was over faster than anyone could have thought. Dominic had been told, several times, by laughing friends, that his wedding would go past in a shocking rush, and he would be lucky to even have the chance to eat a slice of his own wedding-cake.

Speaking of which, the cake *did* look delicious, a towering creation of white icing, marzipan, fruitcake and all sorts of flowers and decorations made out of icing. It was a gift from the Duke, and as such was ridiculously huge and ornate.

He was willing to bet that it was delicious, though.

The day passed in a blur, no matter how hard Dominic tried to hold on. He remembered it later in flashes – the shy smile on Daniella's face as she walked up the aisle in her fine brocade dress, showing him that he was forgiven for punishing her for her rudeness about Ava's doll. Her punishment was not to ride her beloved pony for a full month, which she had accepted with a remarkably good grace. He remembered Steven skipping from foot to foot in entirely too cheerful a manner for a page boy, and Maria's abortive attempt to eat some of the flower petals in her basket.

He remembered Ava, looking so beautiful it took his breath away, before he remembered that their wedding was a ceremony, the opening move in a lifelong partnership in which both of them had clearly defined responsibilities. He glanced away, feeling almost as if he'd betrayed her trust in feeling such things towards her. They had an *agreement*.

The priest droned on while the guests smothered yawns and checked their watches, straightening up in interest when it was time for the *I dos*. Ava and Dominic exchanged rings, cold metal biting into his finger. Hand in hand, they turned to face the crowd and were announced as husband and wife, and Dominic felt almost dizzy.

I am married. Again. I married the woman that I believe I love, but she will never feel the same way about me.

What have I done?

Fortunately, the rest of the day was taken up in tradition and activities, so there was no time to think on his fatal mistake.

There was the wedding breakfast to get through, congratulations to receive, smiles to offer, compliments to listen to, a cake to cut. He remembered the feel of Ava's hand under his, smooth and delicate, as they cut through the cake together, smooth icing and dense fruitcake giving way beneath the blade.

He remembered a strange look in Daniella's face, a sort of misery that made his heart ache, and how she disappeared into the crowd before he could find her. He remembered asking where his children were, and was told that it was late, they were in bed and asleep, and Nurse Emily had taken care of them.

And then it was time for dancing, and of course Ava and Dominic were to open the ball. He led Ava to the centre of the dance floor, they took their positions, looked each other in the eye, and time stopped.

Dominic smiled weakly. "Hello, wife. It seems that I haven't spoken to you all day, except to agree to marry you."

She gave a laugh full of relief and shook her head. "I feel the same. Have you had any of the cake, by the way? It's almost all gone."

"No, but fear not – I asked the butler to save us a couple of slices."

She chuckled again, shaking her head. "How enterprising of you."

The musicians started up the song, and the dance began. Ava and Dominic moved well together, but mechanically, and there was no real heart behind it. Dominic thought he was too tired for real dancing.

And yet time was slowing down, and he began to relax for the first time all day.

"I barely saw the children. I tried to talk to Daniella this morning, but my sisters kept her away from me. I think they were afraid she would do something naughty." Ava commented, idly twirling in Dominic's arms. "I meant to say goodnight to her, but I never did."

"Well, since we aren't having much of a honeymoon, we can start our life right away, right as we mean it to be." He paused. "Are you sure you don't mind it? Not having a honeymoon, I mean? We could take some time off. I don't... don't want you to feel rushed into things. As if you were second best."

Dominic bit his lower lip, willing himself to stop. If she hadn't taken offence before, surely, she would now. But Ava seemed entirely unperturbed.

"Thank you, it's kind of you to say so. But I think I'd rather get started on our married life right away. There's a great deal of things to get right, and I want... I want the children to like me. If I'm to help raise them properly, I'll need to make them like me."

He nodded. It made perfect sense, and it was good to know that she was thinking along the same lines as him.

But then, it was something of a blow to realise just how mercenary their marriage was going to be — omitting a honeymoon, enduring the wedding itself in order to get started on the marriage, the partnership.

This is what I wanted, he reminded himself. *I searched through Society to find a woman who would fit what I was looking for, and who I could offer something to in turn. A woman who wanted a platonic relationship, a friendship, a partnership. No awkwardness, no feelings to make things uncomfortable. That was what I wanted, and it's what I have got.*

I just didn't expect to fall in love with her when I found it.

Dominic stepped back, spinning Ava nimbly, and scattered

applause broke out among the guests. Other couples had joined them at the dance floor by now. There were shy young couples, a little shocked at dancing together at a *wedding* of all places. There were newlyweds, grinning and laughing together. There were older couples, smiling placidly at each other, their dancing sturdy and mechanical rather than graceful, but practised all the same – they had spent decades dancing together.

It made Dominic's heart ache. He wanted nothing more than to sweep Ava into his arms and kiss her, hold her close and tell her that he loved her, that he had just had the good fortune of marrying the woman he loved.

Ha. It was only *good fortune* if one's feelings were requited.

He did no such thing, of course. Even for a married couple, it would be a little shocking. No, *very* shocking. The music drew a close, ending with a flourish.

Dominic released Ava, ignoring the way his heart ached when he did so. He made her a deep, flourishing bow. In return, she sank down into a deep, graceful curtsey, the thick fabric of her skirts pooling around her feet. Applause rose up around them, with people cheering and laughing, and a murmur of conversation broke out while the musicians prepared themselves for the next dance.

Ava and Dominic stood, alone in a crowd, breathless, looking at each other. Dominic could not read her face. Perhaps she was just tired, perhaps she was hungry.

She was his wife, the woman he loved, but she might as well have been a stranger.

Dominic stepped forward and offered his arm.

"Come," he said, still breathless. "Let's have some champagne."

Chapter Twenty

Ava yawned, eyes fluttering open.

It was morning, the sun streaming in. She hadn't been woken – of course not, she had just been married the night before. Dominic and she had politely taken their leave from their wedding celebration at an early hour and travelled back to Dominic's home in silence.

Her new apartments were beautiful, freshly set up for her. A huge bed dominated the bedroom, draped with a silk and velvet canopy, with matching velvet curtains at the window. There was a private washroom, a dressing room, and a neat little receiving room with sofas and a fireplace.

It felt strange, knowing that these rooms were hers.

And, of course, that she was Lady Ava Broughton, wife to the Marquess of Thame. Hm.

Groaning, Ava rolled out of bed. She would need to get settled in her new life as quickly as possible. She would have new duties as lady of the house, and she had better find out what they were, and quickly.

It was almost nine o' clock in the morning, later than Ava preferred to rise. She found herself wondering who would be up at this hour. At home, she knew everyone's routines. Her mother would take breakfast in bed, her father would be up and breakfasted by eight o' clock, and Suzi slept as late as she would be allowed.

Was Dominic awake? Were the children? Perhaps they'd all breakfasted and finished their morning dressing routine already and were now wondering why she was lounging in bed and not getting up.

It wasn't a pleasant thought, so Ava reached over and pulled the bell to summon her maid. She'd better get dressed, and quickly.

"You know, milady, you could have breakfast in bed now," Lizzie commented, doing up the line of tiny buttons on the back of Ava's gown. "You're a married woman now."

Ava sighed. "I don't like the idea of breakfast in bed. Think of all the crumbs."

"I believe there's a tray, your ladyship."

"Even so. Are the children up? What about Lord Thame?"

"Lord Thame takes breakfast in his study, I'm told. He'll be sitting down to it soon, and told the housekeeper that you may join him, if you wish. As to the children, I think they are just being dressed now."

"I'll help the nursemaid dress them," Ava said, more confidently than she felt. She was fairly sure that Steven would be pleased to see her, and probably Maria, but Daniella... Ava cut off that thought with a grimace. There was a great deal of work to be done to make that child like her.

Lizzie pursed her lips in a way that made Ava think that she disagreed, and that nursemaids should be dressing the children and not the lady of the house, but she said nothing.

A few moments later, Ava was picking her way along the maze of corridors in her new home, glad that she'd thought of asking Lizzie the way to the nursery, and wishing she'd listened closer or written down the directions.

Aha, Ava thought with relief, seeing a half-opened door with voices coming from inside. She recognized high-pitched childish voices, and the low chuckle of Nurse Emily.

"But you all enjoyed the wedding celebration, didn't you? Lots of cake and so on," Nurse Emily was saying.

Daniella gave a contemptuous little snort. Ava hovered outside the half-opened door, hating herself for eavesdropping but feeling unable to move away.

"I don't like her," Daniella said stoutly. "And none of you should, either."

"Come, now, Miss Daniella, that's unkind. She's your new mama."

"She is *not* our new mama," Daniella snapped. "Steven, stop crying."

"But I like her, Dannie." Came Steven's mournful voice.

"You're too young to understand, all of you. She's trying to take the place of Mama, plain and simple."

Nurse Emily sighed. "That's not so, Miss Daniella. Besides, your dear, departed mother wouldn't mind you having another lady to care for you. Your papa has chosen well."

"I don't like her," Daniella repeated. "And I'm angry with

you, Nurse Emily. You ought to be on our side. I'm very angry with you."

"What a pity," the nurse said placidly, obviously unmoved by the child's displeasure. "Well, *I* like her, and I think she'll make a fine Lady Thame, whether you let her be your mother or not."

The woman must have crossed the room on noiseless feet, because the door suddenly opened, revealing a guilty Ava in the doorway. She flinched back, blushing, and Nurse Emily lifted her eyebrows. She overcame whatever surprise she felt at seeing Ava standing there and held a finger to her lips.

Nurse Emily moved back along the hallway, gesturing for Ava to follow her.

"I didn't mean to eavesdrop," Ava said in a hushed voice, feeling ashamed. "I just... I just came to help the children get ready for breakfast, and I couldn't help hearing..."

"It's quite alright, Lady Thame, it's your house, after all," Emily said placidly. "I hope you won't take Miss Daniella's words to heart, though. She's a fine child, although she has taken to acting up a little lately."

"I know, I know. She misses her mother dreadfully, doesn't she?"

The nurse nodded. "She feels so deeply. I can't think why she's taken such a dislike to you."

"I can. She thinks I'm trying to take the place of her real mother, and that her mother is going to be forgotten about. I have no intention of doing that, but I can't make her believe me."

Nurse Emily sighed, looking exhausted. "The poor child. If I may drop a word in your ear, Lady Thame – try books."

"Books?"

"Yes, books. Miss Daniella is extremely fond of reading. She has a lot of fine books beside her bed, all presents from her mother. If you mention that, she might be willing to talk about the books. The old Lady Thame used to read to her very night. His lordship does it now."

Ava nodded slowly, thinking. Well, this was something to think about. She liked the idea of Dominic reading bedtime stories to his children and made her feel even closer to him.

Enough of that, my girl, she scolded herself. *But perhaps... perhaps I might use it to my own advantage.*

Aloud, she said, "Thank you, Emily. I appreciate you taking the time to talk to me about this. I know you know these children better than anyone. Thank you."

Nurse Emily gave a smile at that and slipped silently back into the nursery. Alone, Ava walked thoughtfully down the stairs, and was halfway down the hallway before she remembered that she wasn't entirely sure where Dominic's study was.

***

Dominic had his mouth full of bacon and eggs when the tap on the door came, and he only managed an incoherent mumble. The door creaked open, and Ava appeared.

A thrill ran through him, and he was halfway to his feet before he knew it. She waved for him to sit down, chuckling.

"No need to get up from your seat whenever I come into the room, Dominic. We are married now."

"All the more reason for me to get up. I usually take breakfast in my study, and I thought you might like to join me. Unless you have other breakfast plans?"

"No, this is nice. Thank you."

Ava sat down gracefully opposite, helped herself to a plate, and began to serve herself. He watched her for a moment or two before he recalled that it was a little disconcerting to watch someone eat and applied himself to his own breakfast.

"I must say, being a married woman is not much different to being a single one," Ava observed, pouring herself a cup of tea. "Thoughts?"

"Well, I would agree. Of course, ours is more of a partnership than a real marriage."

She flinched when he said that, and Dominic wished he'd kept his mouth shut. Too late now, of course.

"Daniella is still not happy that I am here," Ava said, changing the subject, and went on to tell him how she'd overheard Daniella in the nursery, telling her nurse and her siblings that *she* did not like their new mama and neither should they. He sighed, pressing his lips together.

"I am sorry, Ava. I'll talk to her at once."

"No, don't. That is, it'll just make her like me less. Honestly, I

142

would rather win her over myself. It seems fairer."

Dominic frowned. "Well, we already tried reasoning with her and bribing her. I'm at a loss."

She chuckled, adding marmalade to a piece of toast. "I'm sure there are other ways of reading a child, although of course *you* are the parent."

"What, then? I feel like you have something in mind?"

Ava took her time responding. She ate her toast and took a thoughtful sip of her tea. Dominic found himself waiting, keen to hear what she had to say.

When he was married the first time, he'd had no time believing that he really was married. It had been less complicated, too – no huge house to manage, no fleet of servants, no *children*. But now, with Ava sitting opposite him, he still felt as though they should be chaperoned, as if she should rise at any minute to go home, or *he* should.

It wasn't an unpleasant feeling, just an unfamiliar one.

The hollow feeling inside him remained. He wanted to reach out across the table and take her hand. That would be the sort of casual intimacy a married couple might enjoy, but it wasn't part of their arrangement.

He swallowed hard, almost choking on a piece of scrambled egg. Ava glanced up at him in surprise and mild concern and allowed him to gulp down some water before she responded.

"You read them stories every night, yes?"

"That's right," he managed, throat raw from all the coughing and choking. "What of it?"

She drew in a breath. "I thought I could go and read to them tonight. I intend to spend my day getting familiar with the house, talking with the housekeeper, meeting the servants, and so on, and then you and I can perhaps pay a few calls, if you have time."

"Calls? On the day after our wedding?"

"Well, we don't have to, but I want to go and see Beverley and Suzi, and of course my parents."

"Of course," he echoed, feeling oddly unsettled. "Well, of course if you want to go and read to the children tonight, I can tell you which book we're reading. But I could go and talk to her, if you prefer. It might be simpler."

She sighed, helping herself to another slice of toast. "We are

143

talking about *children,* and when it comes to children, nothing is ever simple."

He winced. "Well, it's hard to argue with that. I know that Daniella is troublesome, but Maria and Steven like you very much."

Ava smiled vaguely. "Yes, and I like them. But Daniella needs attention too, I think."

Dominic found himself struck by how casually she said it. And how easily he believed it – that she cared about Steven and Maria, and about Daniella, even after the way the child had behaved.

She might not love me like I love her, but I chose well, Dominic thought, and allowed himself a small smile.

***

Perhaps it wasn't quite appropriate to hover outside the nursery door and listen in, but Dominic was going to do it anyway. He'd seen Ava slip inside, and Emily had slipped out. The children would be in their night-things and they would be in bed. It was already a full fifteen minutes past their bedtime, but Maria had decided that she no longer liked to go to bed, so it was naturally something of an ordeal to get her, at least, into bed.

Dominic edged closer, peering through the crack of the door. The three beds were laid out at intervals, with a low table beside each. Since Daniella was so fond of books and was such a good reader, she also had a small bookcase.

In pride of place were the gold-spined, leather-bound set of fairytales that had belonged to Marianne. They were a little worse for wear, having been read so often and so thoroughly, but Daniella dusted them herself and kept them neat and clean. For all her faults, she was careful with her things. Dominic's heart ached, and he realised that he hadn't hugged his oldest daughter today.

He could just see Daniella curled up in her bed, turned on her side towards Ava. Ava was sitting on the floor, her back towards the door. From the silence, Dominic guessed that the other two children were asleep, or nearly asleep.

Ava was talking, a low, comforting murmur, and Daniella was listening.

"... and if you like, we can ask your papa about getting you a

144

bigger bookshelf," Ava was saying. "Or perhaps even a corner to yourself in the library?"

Daniella's face brightened at that. "Papa said I was too small to have my own books in the library."

"Yes, but you're older now. I'll speak to him."

"I want to keep Mama's books here."

"Of course. They're such beautiful books, too. Which one is your favourite?"

"I like Hansel and Gretel, although it is so sad."

"Ah, I remember that one. Is it this book? May I take it out and have a look?"

Daniella nodded, and Ava carefully pulled out the book, gently opening the cover.

Dominic had seen enough. Holding his breath, he backed away, suppressing a smile.

Daniella remained unconvinced, far from swayed by any means. She was a stubborn little thing – *she inherited that from me, unfortunately,* he thought sadly – but she seemed happy that Ava was taking an interest in her books.

It's a start, he thought, and hid a smile. He doubted he would see Ava again tonight, unless she joined him in the drawing room. Their lives, it seemed, were going to be separate. The thought made his chest ache more than it should.

You've just seen her act so sweetly with your children, he told himself firmly. *Be grateful, can't you?*

Chapter Twenty-One

My Dearest Sister, Beverley,

I thought I'd write you a little note. Married ladies do keep up correspondence, don't they? Even though we don't live so far away from each other, I have the use of the morning room to myself, and I feel as though the servants are expecting me to be industrious, so here I am, writing a letter.

Was this how you felt when you first were married? Did you feel out of place, and perhaps a little disconcerted? Did you worry what others were thinking about you?

Perhaps it's just me. I have been married for a full week now, and here is how my days usually go.

I take breakfast with Dominic — it feels strange to think of him as my husband — and then we retire to our respective tasks. He has work to keep him occupied, the business of running his estate. If he isn't inundated with paperwork, he has visits to pay and errands to run.

The housekeeper runs the house very neatly, and I don't care to interfere more than I must. She talks over the menu for the day with me so that I may approve her choices, but that is all. The cleaning and maintenance of the house is all done behind the scenes, with no help from me needed at all.

I usually help the children get ready, although Nurse Emily does a good job of that without my help. Daniella seems to have let her resentment for me cool a little, although we are not friends by any stretch of the imagination. Steven and little Maria love me very much, and Maria said she would like to call me Mama if it would not upset Daniella so much.

I told her that she could call me Mama in her head, if she liked, and then Daniella would never know. She seemed pleased with this idea.

And now what, Beverley? There is no chance of me having my own children, and so...

Ava paused, squinting over the last sentence. *No chance of having my own children.* That was true, but perhaps it wasn't an appropriate subject to bring up in a letter.

Sighing, she crumpled the letter into a ball and tossed it into the grate. It was a cool morning, and the fire was set up in the morning-room. A footman had come to lay the fire shortly after Ava had settled down to write, apologizing profusely. It seemed that the previous Lady Thame had used the morning-room for her own business and letter-writing, and they had always set the fire there, except on the hottest of days. They had gotten out of the habit of it, since the room had been mostly abandoned since she had... and there the footman ended the sentence as abruptly as if he'd swallowed his own tongue.

It was almost amusing, as if Ava hadn't known that she had a predecessor or preferred not to think of her.

The flames ate up the abandoned letter, and Ava reached for a fresh sheet of paper.

There was none. The writing-desk was well-stocked, if dusty – it was clear that it hadn't been opened since the last time its previous mistress had used it – and there were no more writing papers. Sighing, Ava got up. She would get fresh supplies from the library.

She thought as she walked, reflecting on her new life, and how odd it felt, like a garment that didn't quite fit.

That's what life is like for us ladies, she thought wryly. *We marry men and are expected to fit into their routines, and their lives don't change at all.*

Perhaps that was an unfair way of thinking about Dominic. He'd been nothing but friendly and courteous.

Like an old great-uncle, making sure you're comfortable, she thought miserably. *Not at all like a husband.*

For the hundredth, if not the thousandth time, she reminded herself that that was their arrangement, and she could hardly complain about it. Then she reached the library and pushed open the door.

She wasn't alone.

Daniella bounced to her feet, holding a comically large book in her hands, seeming guilty.

Ava lifted an eyebrow. "And what are you reading, Daniella?"

"It's... it's about cities of the world," she said nervously, holding up the wordy title, picked out in gold. "There are pictures."

"Ah, I know that book. It's most interesting. Why are you so guilty about reading it?"

Daniella flushed. "Grandpapa said that ladies shouldn't read things about the world and geography. He said it gives them ideas."

Ava snorted. "I should hope it does. Ideas are very fun."

Daniella seemed relieved that Ava was not about to snatch the book away from her and settled back down in her seat.

"Papa won't mind if I read it, will he?" she asked.

"I shouldn't think so. It's good to read books about the world, Daniella. It'll give you a more rounded view of life and of people. It will expand your horizons. Young men often get the chance to travel and see the world, but it's rather frowned upon for a lady to do so."

"I don't care," Daniella insisted stoutly. "I want to go travelling, and I will."

Ava paused, smiling down at the child. "Do you know, I believe that you will. What does your governess say about your books? Has she any recommendations?"

"We don't have a governess."

Ava paused, blinking. "No governess? Why not?"

She shrugged, already lost in her book again. "Papa said that we don't need one yet. Maria is too small, and Steven will go away to school when he's old enough."

"Yes, but a governess can give children a most remarkable start. And what about you, and what about Maria, when she is older?"

Daniella frowned, as if she hadn't much thought about it. "Well, Papa taught us to read, and said that we could read whatever we liked. Grandpapa disagreed, but Papa is good at standing up to him. He said that we should nod and smile at Grandpapa, then do what we want anyway."

At another time, Ava would have been amused, but right now she was focused on the governess business.

"I'm sure your Papa is going to hire one soon," she said, half to herself and half to the little girl.

Daniella barely responded. She was lost in her book, her little mouth sounding out the complicated words. From where she stood, Ava could see the scene that captivated the child. It was a picture of somewhere in China, all colour and gold and swooping, soaring shapes, a place so entirely unlike dull, grey England that it must seem like fairyland to a child.

Ava hid a smile. She was already calculating what tools they would need in the schoolroom – a blackboard, of course, slates, a globe... she would need to do an inventory of the library, to find out what books there were to help a child's learning. And, of course, there would be the business of hiring a governess...

Lost in plans for the future, Ava left the library, entirely forgetting about her notepaper.

***

She tapped on Dominic's study door and waited.

"Who is it?"

"It's me."

"Ah, Ava, come in."

She opened the door, and was greeted by Dominic sitting at his desk, pushing aside his papers. He beamed at her.

"Hello, Ava! I haven't seen you since breakfast. Is everything well?"

"Yes, yes. Do you have a minute to talk?"

"Naturally. I'll ring for tea. Take a seat by the fire, it's a chilly day."

Ava took her seat, letting Dominic bustle around until he sank down into the armchair opposite, and beamed at her.

"Well, what is it, then?"

She drew in a breath. "I wanted to talk about the children's education. Before we were married, you said that you wanted them to be properly educated, yes?"

"Yes, and I do. I have an excellent school lined up for Steven, and..."

"But what about Daniella? She needs a governess."

Dominic sighed. "I suppose so, but she's been so difficult lately. Of course the girls will have to be educated at home, but with Daniella's tantrums and naughtiness... frankly, getting her a governess has been the last thing of my mind. What poor woman would want to teach her?"

"Well, we certainly need to do something about Daniella's

149

behaviour, and not leave it to a governess, but she does need to be *educated*."

"She can read, and she has access to as many of the books in the library as she might want."

Ava paused, thinking it over. "Dominic, you do know that *I* am not a governess?"

He flinched. "Of course, I wasn't implying…"

"And that while I'll do my best to help educate the children, as you will, I don't have the skill to teach them?"

"I know that."

"Which means that we'll have to engage a governess. Daniella seems to think that now Steven has a school picked out for him, you aren't as keen to get them educated."

Dominic looked… well, he looked guilty.

"To be frank," he said after a pause, "I thought I would wait until Maria was a little older, then engage a governess for them both."

"But Daniella is already eight! How much longer do you intend to wait?"

He ran a hand through his hair. "Daniella is just interested in her fairy tales and fiction. She is a bright enough girl, but not scholarly like Steven. She's no fool, but is it really necessary to…"

"I just found Daniella reading *Cities of the World*," Ava interrupted. "She is interested in culture, and literature, and geography, and natural history. Perhaps she doesn't have a flair for mathematics and Latin like Steven, but that doesn't mean that she doesn't need to be educated."

Dominic flushed at that, and Ava realized that she'd hit a nerve.

"What are you implying?" he demanded sharply. "Are you saying that I don't care about my daughters? That I don't think my oldest girl deserves to be educated? Because if you are, Ava, let me tell you that I take great exception to it, and I deny that accusation in the strongest of terms."

She pressed her lips together. "What I am saying is that I, too, had a father who loved me, who taught me to read, but never bothered educating me like he did my brother. Gordon was given the best tutor money could buy and sent to the finest school. He was taught all the modern languages and given the opportunity to learn whatever he liked. He was surrounded by a plethora of erudition, while *I* was set at a pianoforte and taught to entertain, to dance, to be *fascinating*, to paint and display my talents as *accomplishments*. I had access to the library, of course, and I fed my love of natural history and science there. But let me tell you, Dominic, that learning from a book on one's own is a far cry from being properly educated."

He had the grace to blush. Ava drew in a sharp breath, a little shocked at her own outburst.

"You are saying that I don't pay enough attention to my children," he said shortly, and Ava clenched her jaw.

"I am not saying that. Of *course* I am not saying that. But I *am* saying that your daughter has a thirst for knowledge. I know what it's like to be a clever little girl whose cleverness is ignored because she's going to grow up into a woman. It hurts, and don't think she doesn't notice."

Dominic bounced to his feet, and began pacing up and down. "Daniella's behaviour over the past few months has been abominable, and you think she should be rewarded by attention and getting the best education? Is that how you think we should manage this?"

Ava wanted to scream in frustration, or else tear out her own hair by the handful. Was he being deliberately obtuse?

"I am saying that she is dealing with her own growing intelligence, with nowhere to put it, with no outlet. She has nothing to do beyond a few simple exercises with her younger siblings. She needs to stretch her mind like a muscle, and a governess is the way to do that."

Dominic shook his head. He wasn't listening, Ava realised with a sinking heart.

"This is another one of Daniella's ploys, I'm sure of it."

Ava had had enough. She got abruptly to her feet.

"I seem to recall my own father saying something similar. Do excuse me, Dominic."

She strode out of the study, letting the door swing closed behind her. She was aware of Dominic calling after her, but she didn't look back.

Wretched man, she thought venomously. *He's fairly driving me mad. Why can't they just* listen?

Chapter Twenty-Two

Dominic stood where he was for a moment, not entirely sure what had happened.

Was that an argument? Had they just had their first argument? Ugh, he thought so.

Well handled, Dominic, he told himself sourly. *You marry Ava so that she can help you manage your children, and when she makes a perfectly good suggestion, what do you do but dismiss it, and brush it aside?*

Sighing, he moved towards the doorway. He would have to find her and apologise. She was right, really. In fact, if Ava had stayed a few minutes more, she likely would have heard Dominic admit that she was right and apologise to her.

He slipped out into the hallway, where the servants were already putting out some of the candles.

Where would she have gone? He thought, just before rounding the corner and finding himself face to face with Daniella, wearing her nightgown, feet bare.

He flinched, stopping dead.

"Daniella? What are you doing out here? Pray, you shall perilously catch a frigid illness. It's past your bedtime."

Daniella flushed, tilting up her chin and standing her ground.

"I came to talk to you, Papa."

Dominic knelt in front of his daughter, looking thoughtfully into her face. He remembered what he'd said to Ava about the girl's education, and a flush of shame rose to his cheeks.

I'm sorry, darling, he thought wryly. *I'll do better. I will, I promise.*

"What is it, Daniella? Tell me quickly, and then I'll tuck you back into bed."

Daniella shifted from foot to foot, looking a little nervous.

"Well... well, it's about Sylvie, Papa."

He frowned. "Your pony? You know you aren't allowed to ride her till the end of the month, Daniella. You know why, too. You were extremely rude and unkind to Ava when she gave you a lovely gift."

Dominic still cringed inside at the memory of that tea party.

He knew, now, why Daniella was so upset about the gift of what seemed to be a beautiful, expensive doll in a brocaded dress. However, he also knew that Ava hadn't intended any harm at all – quite the reverse. Daniella's doll sat neatly on her bookshelf, and while she did not play with it like her brother and sister played with their gifts, Dominic often caught her looking wistfully at it, fingering the hem of the ornate, brocaded doll's dress.

He knew that deep down Daniella felt sorry for her outburst, and had even made an apology to Ava, of sorts. Still, it wouldn't do to let her say and do what she liked without any consequence and keeping her from doing something she enjoyed very much seemed like a good punishment.

Daniella fidgeted from foot to foot. "Yes, Papa, but it's been so very long, and I *am* sorry. Sylvie will be very sad and bored in the stables without me."

"Don't worry, dear, Sylvie is being cared for properly. One of the stable lads takes her on a ride every day."

After all, the poor pony was not being punished.

Daniella did not seem happy at this. "But Papa, she's *my* pony. I want to ride her, please."

He patted her cheek. "And so you will, but not until the end of the month. That's what we talked about, and you know that you are being punished. I'm sorry, but I must stick to my word. You wouldn't have me go back on what I said, would you?"

Daniella's little face was pink with annoyance, and she turned on her heel and raced away down the hall towards her room, white nightdress fluttering. Dominic got to his feet, wondering if he should go after. After a moment, he decided against it. He would only wake the others, if she'd gone to bed. They could discuss it in the morning.

One thing Dominic was determined on, though, and that was not to reduce Daniella's punishment. He wasn't about to strike his children, or take away their meals or something like that, but she had behaved very badly and had had multiple warnings. It was a fair punishment.

In the end, he found Ava in the library.

The library was a fine room, situated to overlook the terrace, with the low shape of the stables across the way. It got plenty of light during the day, obliging them to turn the bookshelves away from the window to avoid the covers fading.

There was a long window-seat, well padded, and that was where Ava sat, feet tucked underneath her and face turned towards the moonlit courtyard.

She glanced up as he entered and sighed to herself.

"I've come to apologise..."

"I think I owe you an apology..."

They both began at the same time and stopped at the same time.

Blinking, Ava leaned forward, uncurling her legs from underneath her, eyeing him curiously.

"*You* came to apologise?" she said, somewhat incredulously.

"Yes," he said, with a short laugh. "I should be apologising, I think we both know that. You came to me with a good suggestion, and I dismissed it. So, I am sorry, Ava."

She eyed him for a long moment, then gave a long exhale, patting the seat beside her.

He took it wordlessly, and for a moment or two, they sat side by side, back to the window, facing into the buttery, candle-lit interior of the library.

It might be a beautiful and well-lit room during the day, but once the sun had gone down, it turned into a dark maze, where you were more likely to strain your eyes than actually enjoy your reading experience.

"Perhaps I should have said it all a bit differently," Ava said absently, after a long moment. "Instead of barging into your study and demanding that you do things differently. I haven't even had a long talk with Daniella to ask about what sort of education she would like."

He shook his head. "No, you did right. I've been so wrapped up in making Daniella into a perfect little lady that I entirely forgot about my plans to educate my children *properly*. Steven is easy to manage – he naturally enjoys studying, and a proper school will educate him. Maria is too young for me to worry about these things, but Daniella – well, time is precious at her age, and I'm letting time slip away. I *should* be engaging a governess, and a good one. I can afford the best. I can afford a finishing school for her, too, if she wants to be a proper lady – although times are changing, and I'm not sure that singing and pianoforte playing at musical evenings will be as important to a lady's future as they are now."

Ava winced. "Oh, don't remind me. A girl is told that if she can't sing, can't dance perfectly, can't play pianoforte or paint or embroider cushion covers, if she doesn't memorize every rule in the game, we call Society and play the game well, she can forget about any sort of happiness in life. Strangely enough, following all the rules makes a person *less* likely to be happy, not more so. I... I know that Daniella is not my daughter, but I don't want that life for her. Truly, I don't. I want her to be happy, self-sufficient, and to be able to think differently to what *Society expects*. And she can't have that without an education."

Dominic nodded slowly, a lump rising to his throat. He had a memory of Marianne, sitting with baby Daniella on her knee.

"She," Marianne had said, grinning, *"is going to be able to think for herself, Dom. I can wager you that."*

And he'd so nearly thrown away the opportunity.

"You're right," he managed at last. "You're right. If Daniella is going to be able to keep her feet in this world, she'll need to be educated. Tomorrow, we'll talk over what sort of governess we need to hire. We can ask around, to see if any of our friends know somebody suitable. If not, we'll write a concise advertisement in a few genteel papers, and see what comes of it."

On impulse, he reached down to where her hand lay on the window seat between them and placed his hand over it. He sensed, rather than heard, her sharp intake of breath. She glanced up at him, but in the darkness, it was almost impossible to make out her expression.

"We'll interview the candidates together," he said firmly. "You and me. We'll talk to Daniella and tell her what is happening. We'll make sure she behaves for the governess, but if you're right about her needing to... to exercise her mind like a muscle, I think that having an outlet will do her a great deal of good. And Steven can be educated too, to get a head start on school, and so can Maria, once she's old enough. You've already made such progress with the children. Steven and Maria adore you already, and Daniella... well, I think that Daniella is growing to respect you at the very least, and that's an excellent start."

There was a moment of silence after his little speech, and

Ava let out a long breath.

"Thank you," she said softly, at last, and he shivered. His hands still lay on hers, the warmth of their skin melding together.

"Why are you thanking me? We are meant to be partners in all this. I hoped that at least we could be friends."

"Friends," she repeated, and the word was a half-breath, barely heard. He did hear it, though, and it shivered.

When had they moved so close together? Their shoulders were almost brushing, and the folds of Ava's gown touched Dominic's knee. She was still watching him, her eyes bright and liquid in the gloom. She was lit from behind by blue-silver moonlight, and from in front by the old-yellow candlelight, flames bouncing and throwing deep shadows across the room and across Ava's face.

Dominic realised that he was holding his breath and let it out with a gasp.

"Yes," he managed, realising that some response was expected. "Friends. We are friends, aren't we?"

"Certainly, certainly," Ava responded, looking away. The spell was broken, and Dominic found himself missing the strange feeling which had kept him pinned in place.

She hadn't moved her hand, though. On impulse, he reached into his pocket, searching for the little cloth-wrapped bundle he had kept in his pocket ever since he bought it.

"I... I have something for you, Ava. A sort of wedding-present, if you like. I haven't quite had the courage to give it to you yet, as I feel that it means... oh, I'm being ridiculous."

She glanced back at him, eyes unreadable, and her eyebrows inched higher.

"You seem a little out of sorts, Dominic. Is everything alright?"

"What? Oh, yes, yes. Although I did just meet Daniella out in the hallway, and she was trying to convince me to transmute her punishment. I did expect this, but it's a little hard to look her in her face and tell her that she can't ride Sylvie until the end of the month."

Ava gave a short laugh. "Yes, you're not an unkind parent. You're a good man, Dominic. The best. A little too soft-hearted, I'd say."

"I'm not sure whether that's a compliment or an insult."

"I think you know exactly which one it is."

They chuckled together, and Dominic's hand tightened around Ava's. She threaded her fingers through his, shifting so that they were palm to palm.

She didn't look away. Dominic had touched the cloth parcel in his pocket, but made no move to look away, either. He felt as though he were transfixed.

"Ava, I..." he began, but broke off, a lump rising to his throat and threatening to choke him. Ava's breath was short and ragged, and she lifted a hand to his face. Soft fingertips grazed his cheek, sending tingles of sensation along his skin, making his spine shiver. She was watching him so intently, the space between them closing, closing, closing... he dropped his gaze down to her lips, almost incredulous.

"Ava..." he said again, the name barely more than a breath.

He could feel her warm breath ghosting across his cheek, could almost feel the tickle of her hair on his forehead.

And then a scream split the air, and they leapt apart as if they'd been burned.

Ava's eyes widened, and she sucked in a long, ragged breath.

"Dominic, did you..."

A second scream came, unmistakably a child's voice. Dominic glanced across the terrace and saw a light on in the stables, a single square window illuminated.

He gave a choked gasp. "It's Daniella," he managed.

Chapter Twenty-Three

Ava and Dominic raced along the halls to the French doors, which opened out onto the terrace below the library window, and from there led to the stables, if one cut across the lawn.

Already, some of the servants had noticed that something was wrong, with footmen peering anxiously out through the windows, murmuring between themselves. They leapt back at the sight of their master and mistress, eyes widening with fear when they took in Dominic's face, white with panic.

"Where is Nurse Emily?" Dominic gasped.

Fear pulsed through him in time to his heartbeat. Wild and horrible imaginings appeared in his mind's eye.

Stop it, you fool, he chastised himself. *Just because you hear a child's scream doesn't mean that Daniella is in danger. It could be one of the younger scullery maids, or a local child, or... or... well, at any rate, soon Emily will come and report that all three children are safe and sound in bed, and I've worried myself almost to death for nothing.*

And then a footman appeared, with a breathless Nurse Emily behind him. She looked pale and strained.

"I was in my room, your lordship, since the children were all in bed..." she began, stammering. "I went to check on them, and Miss Daniella is gone. She's gone, sir!"

Beside him, Ava gave a moan of fear. She darted past Dominic, whose feet seemed to have rooted themselves to the ground, and out onto the cool, moonlit terrace.

He followed her, with a cluster of servants following, heading by Nurse Emily.

The stables were rarely used by the family. Dominic could ride, of course, and he assumed that Ava could too, but he didn't particularly enjoy riding for pleasure. He wasn't a hunting man, either. The stables were a place where the estate's horses were kept and cared for, by a handful of diligent and experienced grooms. Out of them all, only Daniella went into the stables to help saddle up her beloved Sylvie. The stable lads and grooms all knew that she wasn't permitted to ride for a month and wouldn't go against Dominic's requirements.

However, it was possible that Daniella could saddle up her own horse.

Dominic felt sick.

Ava barged through the stable doors, which were worryingly ajar. Inside, the place was heavy with the smell of horses and hay, with the creatures all standing sedately in their respectable stalls.

Except one, of course. The stall with *Sylvie* painted on the door stood open and empty, and Dominic immediately glanced over Ava's shoulder, out through the double doors which led into the large paddock. From the paddock, where a horse could be sedately walked around in large circles, there were gates which opened out onto the rest of the world.

Ava stood where she was, breathing heavily, and Dominic pushed past her, heading out into the paddock.

The lighting out here was poor, with only a single lantern burning by the door, which did almost nothing to illuminate the hard-packed courtyard. Aside from that, he had to rely on moonlight and starlight covering the world with a glittering, cold illumination.

He spotted Sylvie at once, the dutiful little pony, all saddled up and ready to go, trotting briskly around the paddock, huffing and tossing her head, ears pinned tightly back.

Nobody sat on her back. Dominic spotted a large white cat, back arched and claws flashing out, hissing angrily at the pony. Perhaps that was what scared her, then – Sylvie was a good pony, but a little nervy at times.

And then he spotted the dark, motionless shape in the shadows, roughly the size and shape of a small girl.

Fear surged up Dominic's throat, tasting like bile, and he went racing over to her, skidding the last few feet on his knees.

Behind him, Ava squinted in the poor light, and he heard her give a cry of alarm.

"Fetch the doctor," he heard her say, through the roaring in his ears. "Fetch the doctor immediately."

Dominic reached his little girl, scarcely daring to touch her in case she was already dead and cold. Of course she wouldn't be, not after such a short time, but he was not thinking rationally. Of course he was not.

He spotted a nasty gash above her forehead, blood matting

her hair and trickling down her cheek. She whimpered, and her eyes cracked open.

"Papa?" Daniella rasped. "Papa, I'm sorry, I know I shouldn't have done, but... but Sylvie was so pleased to see me... then there was a cat that scared her... she threw me... Papa, my head aches."

Dominic felt dizzy. He glanced over his daughter, looking for any other injuries. As if her head wound was not enough.

"That doesn't matter, dearest. What else hurts, beside your head? Can you move your arms and legs?"

Daniella made her hands and feet twitch, although her little face crumpled with pain. Her eyes were dull and unfocused, and kept wanting to roll back in her head, although she was struggling to keep them open.

Ava dropped to her knees beside Dominic, reaching for Daniella.

"Are you hurt?" she gasped. "Are you hurt, my love."

Daniella's blank gaze focused on Ava. "Why are you so kind to me?"

That was all she managed. Before either Ava or Dominic could respond, Daniella's eyes rolled back into her head, and she began to twitch and spasm violently, going into a fit of sorts. Ava shrieked, backing away with her hands pressed over her mouth, while Dominic tried to stop the girl banging her head or scraping her skin on the ground.

The fit only lasted for half a minute, but Dominic knew that there was no time to waste. As soon as Daniella's little frame relaxed, he swept her up into his arms and staggered to his feet.

"We need to get her inside," he said, somewhat unnecessarily. "Not in the nursery. Where shall we put her?"

"In the late Lady Thame's room?" someone suggested. "It's all made up."

"No!" Dominic yelped, almost reeling at the prospect of putting his daughter in the bed his first wife had died in. "No, absolutely not!"

"Put her in my room," Ava said, with flawless sensibility. Casting her a quick grateful look, Dominic hurried across the paddock, holding Daniella tightly to his chest, as if he were afraid that she would fade away if he didn't hold her firmly enough.

***

It took over two hours for the doctor to arrive, since he had been out to dine at the time, and it had taken a while for the message to reach him.

Dominic sat in a seat in the hallway outside of Ava's room. Mrs Silo was in and out with cups of lemon tea and honey, and a few plain pieces of bread and butter which were not eaten. There was something of a commotion downstairs, but Dominic could not rouse himself to get up and see what was going on. He sat where he was, staring at the wood of the closed door, and did not even turn when he heard footsteps approaching.

"Forgive my lateness," came the clipped tones of Doctor Figg. "I came as soon as I could."

"I know," Dominic managed, which really didn't seem enough, given the circumstances.

"I understand the little girl took a tumble from a horse? How bad was the impact?"

"We... we don't know. She wasn't permitted to ride for a while, as a punishment for... well, it hardly matters now. She's not allowed to ride with out a groom to watch her, and she snuck out to ride alone. We weren't there. If we hadn't heard her scream, she might have lain there all night."

The bleak, blunt description of the facts made the situation seem worse than ever. Dominic tore his eyes away from the closed door and glanced up at Doctor Figg, a neat little man who looked exactly like a doctor *ought* to look, with his greying hair, pointed beard, and pince-nez perched on his nose.

"I should have been watching her," he managed, brokenly.

Doctor Figg shook his head. "You mustn't think that way. This is an unpleasant accident. This is not your fault. Where is Lady Thame?"

"She's nursing her. I was too, but I... I needed a moment."

Needed a moment to think about what a terrible parent I am.

Doctor Figg gave another crisp nod and slipped into the bedroom without another word.

Dominic should have gotten up and gone in after him, but he felt numb again, as if he were frozen to the seat.

What will I do if Daniella dies? Our oldest girl, our pride and joy? He closed his eyes, remembering the look of mingled wonder and pride on Marianne's face as she held their first baby. He remembered his own feelings of fear and excitement, holding a tiny bundle that was *theirs* in a way that nothing else had ever been.

He heard murmured voices inside the room, and finally, slowly, forced himself to his feet and forward.

Ava's room was disarranged, naturally. Things were strewn everywhere, shoved in corners and forgotten about in the panic over the little girl. Mrs Silo and two maids stood off to one side, dabbing their eyes with handkerchiefs and whispering.

Doctor Figg stood on one side of the huge bed, and Ava on the other, both wearing matching expressions of grim resignation. Ava was holding one of Daniella's hands, as if for comfort, and Doctor Figg was mirroring her, fingers on the little girl's wrist to take her pulse.

Daniella lay in the middle, face bone white, eyes closed, lying on her back, entirely still. Her hair hung lank around her face, spreading out on the pillow, and a lumpy bandage was wound around her temples. Doctor Figg was speaking to Ava in a low, serious voice, and trailed off as Dominic appeared.

He sighed, shaking his head and not meeting Dominic's eyes.

"It's not good, is it?" Dominic heard himself say. His voice sounded thin and exhausted. What time was it? It felt like midnight, but it could not be later than eight or nine o' clock.

"No," Doctor Figg said crisply. The man's bedside manner was not the best, but Dominic knew from experience that he was a skilled doctor, and never one to muddy the facts or hide the truth. "No, it is not, Lord Thame. The head injury is a singular one, and there is not a great deal I can do. She is concussed, I think. She ought not to have slept after the accident, but of course you were not to know that, and I was not here."

"So, what can we do?" Ava said, when it was clear that Dominic could not manage to speak.

Doctor Figg sighed again, looking down at the little girl with something like regret.

"We must wait. A fever is rising, and it will break during the night, I think. I cannot stay – there is a troublesome birth I must

163

oversee in one of the farmer's homes, and there is nothing I could do for the poor child even if I did stay. Watch her, keep her comfortable, try and keep her temperature down, and... well, pray, I suppose."

"And... and that's it?" Dominic managed. His mouth was dry. When had he last had a drink of anything? He wanted nothing more than a cup of tea, but the idea of ordering tea when his child lay senseless in bed felt sickening.

"I'm afraid so," Doctor Figg finally met his eye. "I'm sorry, Lord Thame. All we can do is wait, and hope. I'll leave a cooling draught for her to take, if she can. This is going to be a long night. I'll come as soon as I am finished with the farmer's wife, but you should not expect me before dawn. I am sorry."

With that, he gently placed Daniella's limp hand back on the sheets, closed up his bag with a *snap* that made Dominic flinch, and moved quietly past him and out into the hallway.

"She's going to die," Dominic heard himself say. "She's going to die. Oh, Ava..."

Ava moved around the bed and put her arms around him, holding him tight.

"She won't die, Dominic. She won't."

"How can you know that? You saw the doctor's face. A fever is what carried off Marianne, at the end. Oh, Ava, how could I have been so foolish? This is all my fault."

Ava pulled back, putting her hands on either side of his face, forcing him to look at her.

"It is *not* your fault," she said fiercely. "And we will not let Daniella die, not if earthly efforts can prevent it. Now, you sit by her, and keep a close eye on her, while I make some arrangements."

Ava immediately turned to Mrs Silo.

"We need bowls of cool, fresh water, and rags. We need drinking water, and perhaps a sponge to dribble water between her lips if she won't drink. Tea for us – we'll need to keep up our strength – and perhaps some refreshments, too."

Mrs Silo sniffed back tears, putting away her handkerchief. A businesslike air came over her – Ava's determination, it seemed, was catching.

"As you say, Lady Thame. We'd like to stay up with you.

We're all fond of Miss Daniella, and Nurse Emily is quite taken up with the other two children."

Ava gave an approving nod. "Excellent. I would value your help, all of you. Prepare tea and refreshments for yourselves, too. Miss Daniella's nightclothes and perhaps a hairbrush — we'll make her comfortable, if we can. No, wait, I shall fetch them myself."

And just like that, the women scattered, each going to her task, and Dominic was left alone by his daughter's bedside, wild with fear and worry. He crawled onto the bed beside Daniella and lay down, reaching over to smooth hair back from her hot, sticky face.

"Stay alive for me, darling," he whispered hoarsely. "Please, please do."

Chapter Twenty-Four

It was a relief to have something to do. Ava hated feeling helpless, especially since there was already so little for them to do. She walked quickly down the carpeted corridors, trying not to remember how small and frail Daniella looked under the blankets, or the way sweat was already starting up on her dangerously waxy skin.

Or the blank-eyed look of grief of Dominic's face.

Drawing in a deep breath and reminding herself of what needed to be done, Ava eased open the nursery door.

The lights were all on, of course. The commotion had unsurprisingly woken the other children, and Ava hadn't expected Nurse Emily to get them back to bed just yet.

She was right. Steven was out of bed, looking younger than ever in his large nightgown, clutching at Emily's skirts. Maria was balanced on Emily's hip, her face half-buried in Rabbit Alice.

All three of them looked up as Ava entered, and Steven went scuttling over to her.

"Ava, Ava, what is wrong with Daniella? Nobody will tell us," he asked hopefully. "Is she ill?"

A kind lie danced on the tip of Ava's tongue. Then she met Emily's eye over Steven's head, and her shoulders sank. She knelt down before Steven to look him in the eye.

"I'm afraid that Daniella is rather ill. She's had an accident – she fell, you see. The doctor is coming back soon, and your papa and I are going to take care of her until then."

Steven's lower lip pushed out. "I want to see her."

"You can't, my dear. Maria and you need to go back to sleep, and in the morning, I'm sure Daniella will be recovered. Or we will at least have some news for you."

Steven shook his head. "I can't sleep. I'm scared."

Ava's heart ached. She wrapped her arms around Steven, pulling him close in a tight hug.

In an instant, she was transported back to her teen years, when a teary-eyed Suzi would come tiptoeing into her room in the middle of the night, driven by fear of some nightmare or childish worry. Back then, Ava would roll her eyes, pretending to be

166

annoyed, and move over so that Suzi could slide into bed beside her.

Steven put his small arms around her neck and held her tight.

"I don't want Daniella to die," he said, his voice muffled. "I was annoyed with her and didn't say goodnight before we went to bed. I wish I had."

She swallowed hard. "Well, whatever happens, we'll all face it together as a family, won't we?"

Steven pulled back, his little face red with worry and tears. "Promise?"

"Promise," she agreed.

She rose to her feet, pressing a kiss to the top of Steven's head, and glanced at Emily.

"I need a nightdress for Daniella, perhaps a brush, and some more linens."

Emily gave a crisp nod. "One of her books, perhaps? It might soothe her, to be read to."

"That's a good idea, Emily, thank you. Take care of the children tonight, won't you?"

Emily nodded again. "Of course, Lady Thame. And... and take care of Miss Daniella, won't you?"

Ava met her gaze and held it. "I will, Emily. I promise."

Dominic met her at the bedroom door when she returned. His jacket was gone, his waistcoat unbuttoned, and his sleeves rolled up. His hair was dishevelled, as if he'd been running his hands through it.

"The fever is rising," he said, breathless. "She's getting worse, Ava."

Ava drew in a breath. "It's going to be a long night."

***

Daniella's fever reached its crisis in the cold, dark hour before dawn.

As promised, Mrs Silo stayed up all night, sending the maids to bed one by one and overriding their protests.

Fresh bowls of water were brought, and cool rags placed on Daniella's wrists and neck. They seemed to work, but so sooner had her temperature retreated to something normal, it would shoot up again, and her colour would heighten unnaturally.

Half a dozen times during the night, Ava thought that it was all over. And half a dozen times, Daniella would doggedly pull through the crisis, sinking back into the mattress as if exhausted.

"She's stubborn," Dominic said once, tears drying on his cheeks. "She gets that from me."

The final crisis had the three of them racing around in panic, opening windows, begging Daniella to just keep breathing, to just hold on until morning, just a little longer, just until dawn.

Occasionally, during the quiet moments, Ava and Dominic would take turns to take the air outside the stifling room, to pace up and down the corridors.

There was no light coming from underneath the nursery, Ava noticed, and no sound from inside. Nurse Emily's room, however, which opened up onto the nursery, let out a thin beam of light from underneath, and if she stopped and listened, she could hear the slow, regular scrape of pages turning.

Daniella's fever broke along with the dawn.

The child lay weak and shivering, wound up in tangled, sweaty blankets, and her eyes cracked open for the first time, glancing at first her father and then at Ava.

"Hello, darling," Dominic whispered, his voice half-choked. "You're awake."

"I'm thirsty, Papa."

At once, Ava had a cup of water placed at Daniella's lips, and she took grateful sips. She would have drunk the whole thing in a few large gulps, but Ava was careful to only let her drink the water in gradual, small sips, to avoid throwing it all back up again.

Outside, a light rattling came up the drive, and an exhausted-looking Mrs Silo moved to the window, pulling back the curtain to peer out.

"It's Doctor Figg," she announced, clearly too tired to bother with any formalities. Ava and Dominic were too tired to care.

Ava got to her feet, smoothing down her hopelessly wrinkled gown. "Thank you for everything you have done, Mrs Silo. You must be exhausted. Please, go to bed – Daniella is out of danger for now. The night footman will bring Doctor Figg up. You need your rest."

Mrs Silo nodded, passing a tired hand over her face. As she moved past the bed towards the door, Dominic reached out, taking her hand.

"Thank you," he said simply.

She looked at him for a long moment, then nodded wordlessly. She moved past, and Dominic and Ava were left alone.

"Thank you, too," Dominic said, after a pause. "If you hadn't been here… I don't know what I would have done."

"You would have done what needed to be done," Ava responded. "She's your daughter, and you know what to do. Didn't you see the way she calmed down when you read to her?"

Daniella was sleeping now, a proper sleep, not the fevered unconsciousness of earlier. Ava felt like crying, out of exhaustion, relief, or both, she had no idea.

Footsteps echoed along the hallway, and the door opened to admit Doctor Figg and, to Ava's surprise, Emily.

Emily met Ava's gaze and smiled wryly. "I couldn't sleep," she said, by way of explanation.

"Extraordinary," Doctor Figg murmured, moving over to the bedside. He checked Daniella's vitals, tested her temperature, and seemed pleased by what he found.

"I'd say she's out of danger," he said, relief in his voice. "You have done well. She still needs to be watched, but she is sleeping, and that is a good sign."

"I'll stay up with her," Emily spoke up. "Lord and Lady Thame had been up all night with her. They're exhausted. I would like to take my turn."

She glanced at Ava and Dominic as if for approval. Ava glanced at Dominic, and he gave the smallest of nods.

"Very well," Doctor Figg said, having followed the exchange. "Nurse Emily and I can watch the child for a few hours, and you two may sleep. I daresay it's been a trying night for everyone."

"You have no idea," Dominic muttered, but not loud enough for anyone but Ava to hear. They filed outside, and the door was closed behind them, and it was over.

And then they were standing, face to face, in the hallway outside Ava's room, and suddenly she had everything to say and nothing at all.

"Well," she began, at the same moment that Dominic said, "I

suppose that..."

They both stopped, clearing their throats.

Ava was suddenly aware of how untidy she looked. How untidy they *both* looked. Dominic's eyes were heavy, his hair falling into his eyes. Ava's hair had long since come undone from its fine style, and she'd hastily retied it into a long, lumpy plait. She probably looked dead on her feet.

"Thank you," he said quietly. "For being there. And I have something for you, I'd like to give it you now. I meant to give it to you earlier, and perhaps now is not the right time, but... well, here it is."

He withdrew a small, cloth-wrapped parcel from his pocket and handed it to her. She took it, curiously weighing the thing in her hand. It wasn't heavy. Dominic leaned back against the wall, waiting for her to look at it. She unwrapped it, undoing layers of cloth and tissue paper until finally she revealed a ring.

It wasn't like the simple, plain gold bands they'd exchanged on their wedding day. This ring was made of silver, cunningly engraved with flowers and vines, with a neat green stone in the centre, curled around with carved silver leaves.

It was beautiful.

"It's lovely," Ava said, and meant it. "But you have already given me so much jewellery."

He smiled wryly. "I know, but I wanted this to mean something. I... I must speak to you about this, Ava. I've been putting it off for a while, but what happened tonight made me see how much I value you, and how quickly something can be taken away."

Shivers ran down Ava's spine. "What do you mean?"

"I mean that I love you, Ava," he said flatly. She drew in a sharp, surprised gasp.

"I... you..."

"I offered you a wedding ring because I liked you, and I liked your qualities, and I thought that you would fit well into my family. That you would be a good mother to my children," he continued, meeting her gaze and holding it. "Those were my reasons. I don't pretend to know yours, but I know you had your own reasons to marry me. It was meant to be a business-like arrangement, a partnership at worst, a friendship at best. But I've come to realise that I want more than that from you, Ava. I love you. I want a real marriage."

There was a pause, which would have been the ideal time for Ava to speak. But her tongue didn't seem to want to work, so Dominic continued.

"Now, I'm aware of what we intended when we agreed to marry. If your sentiments haven't changed, then I'll never speak to you about this again. We'll go on as we were before, as friends and partners. But I had to tell you how I felt, at the very least. I love you, Ava. I'm giving you this ring to symbolise a true marriage beginning – if that's what you want. Naturally, if you want to go on as we are, you can still keep the ring," he added, with a wry smile.

Ava found her voice.

"Marrying you, Dominic, was the best thing I ever did," she murmured, and saw hope light up in his eyes. "I never dared think too deeply about my feelings, because it wasn't what we'd agreed, but…" she closed her fingers over the ring. "But I love you too, Dominic. I love the children, and we agreed to marry for the right reasons, but if I am honest with myself, I think I married you because I loved you."

He sucked in a breath, and Ava barely had time to smile up at him before he caught her in his arms, pulling her close to him and kissing her.

She wrapped her arms around his neck, nearly dropping the ring in the process, and wound the fingers of her free hand into the soft hairs at the base of his neck. There was nothing except the two of them, nothing in the world….

And then muffled voices came from behind the closed door at Ava's back, and they jolted apart, red-faced.

"I suppose I should have asked Mrs Silo to make up a spare room for me," Ava managed, breathless all of a sudden. "No matter. I'll find somewhere."

Dominic swallowed hard. "Well, if you liked – only if you liked – you could share my room. We are married, after all. It would hardly be improper."

Heat rose to Ava's face, but she managed a smile.

"I think that would certainly be the best thing to do."

He extended a hand, and she took it without a beat of hesitation. The two of them made their slow way along the corridor, although Ava had to admit that the weariness seemed to have gone from her frame now, evaporated along with the rising sun.

Strange, indeed.

Epilogue

Six Months Later

Dedicated readers will recall the shocking circumstances of the departure of Mrs Ursula Winslow, a dashing widow with a remarkable fortune and great charm, from polite Society to the Continent. While Mrs Winslow's departure was greatly bemoaned, it must be admitted that certain stories surfaced after that lady's departure which threw aspersions on her otherwise spotless character.

While gossips have concluded that Mrs Winslow's sudden departure was connected with the unorthodox marriage between Lady Ava Devane and Lord Thame – who was commonly thought to have been a Conquest of Mrs Winslow – the author must admit that the unusual match between the spinster and the eligible widower has resulted in, to all outward appearance, happiness.

News of Mrs Winslow's marriage to Count Ortensky – a Russian gentleman who is unknown to London Society – was said to be a remarkable match, and many of us hoped that the Count and Countess would visit our modest London and give the gossips something to talk about.

The Count is said to be a somewhat infamous man – with rather austere tastes, and a reputation for... shall we say, unpleasantness? ...in his local sphere. Of course, it is to be remembered that the author of this publication lives here, in England, as such we are limited in what we can find out regarding foreign nobility and their proclivities. It should also be noted that various cultures and customs abound in different nations, and this author is not ascribing traditional English beliefs to a different culture – one must be open-minded *in these modern times.*

However, it seems that the newlyweds are not *enjoying wedded bliss. Rumours of arguments, paid-off servants, and a general nasty atmosphere have been reported in the Count's castle, set in the rural parts of Russia – the author apologises for such vague terms, but one must do one's best. If rumours are to be believed, the Countess has in fact left her husband and gone to France. She is said to have left with a secretary employed by the*

Count himself, and their whereabouts are unknown. If this is true, this author does not know whether the Count intends to take back his Countess, or whether he would prefer to cut his losses and move on. For shame, Countess Ortensky, for shame!

As always, more details will be revealed when this author discovers them.

In the meantime, alas, we must urge young women and men to beware – beware of wealthy and intriguing Russian counts and beware of dangerously charming widows!

Ava pursed her lips and set aside the scandal sheet. She hated reading the things, but it was practically required reading for a person to manage in Society. She'd heard plenty of rumours about Ursula Winslow in the previous half-year, but reading about the woman in the scandal sheets didn't please her as much as she thought it might.

In fact, it seemed sad.

"Ava?" Dominic peered into the drawing room. "There you are. Aren't you coming outside? It's a fabulous day, and I'm about to pour out the champagne. Willi is asking about you." He paused, glancing down at the scandal sheet, abandoned on the table. "Oh, were you reading that nonsense?"

"Yes, I can't help it," Ava sighed. "Ursula Winslow has gotten herself into trouble again. I should feel pleased, especially considering I *know* she was behind those awful articles about us. But I only feel sad."

Dominic came properly into the room, and put his arms around her, pulling her close. She rested her head on his shoulder and closed her eyes.

"You're too kind, my love," he murmured. "I'm glad you're not pleased, though. You've never been the spiteful type."

He kissed the top of her head, and Ava let herself lean against him. It felt strange to think that Ursula Winslow and she had been in competition for Dominic. The Count that Mrs Winslow had married in the end couldn't possibly have been anywhere near as wonderful as Dominic. Even the sight of him could make Ava's heart beat faster. She suppressed a smile and moved back.

"We'd better go outside," she said, almost apologetically. "You're right, I've been in here too long. What *will* our guests think of us?"

Outside, picnic blankets had been spread over the lawn, with hampers and goodies everywhere. The children were causing chaos, naturally – Maria was trying to convince Suzi that a mud pie would taste just as nice as a real one, and Richard and Steven were playing diligently with Steven's wooden animals. Willi sat beside the two of them, watching Richard with a strange expression on his face. As Ava approached, she saw Richard glance up, more than once, and his gaze immediately slid Willi's way.

She fought not to smile. This was an interesting development, but it would be best to see where it went.

Daniella was mostly recovered from her accident. She was still a little weak – her recovery had been slow, after that first horrible night and her sudden spurt of strength – but she was getting better, day by day. *She* was sitting beside Beverley, with the baby resting in her lap.

Ava found a space beside her sister and Daniella and leaned over to smile at the baby.

"Little Frederick is getting bigger every time I see him," she commented, and Beverley snorted.

"Yes, babies do that, you silly goose. It's hard to believe he's a month old already."

"I think he's lovely," Daniella said stoutly, earning a pleased look from Beverley. "I'm allowed to hold him, Ava. Aunt Beverley said so."

Beverley – who was quite enjoying her new title of *aunt* – gave a nod.

"She's a natural with him."

Ava nodded, flashing a quick smile at Daniella, which was immediately returned.

Since that awful night where she had been so sure that Daniella would die, the atmosphere in the house had changed. Steven and Maria seemed to believe that Ava had brought Daniella back from the brink of death by sheer willpower alone and treated her accordingly.

Sometimes, Ava thought that Daniella and Dominic thought so, too.

Daniella began to talk, babbling away about everything and nothing, from the baby to her pony – which she was still not permitted to ride, although it was accepted that Sylvie had not been at fault over the whole incident – and the adults settled back to listen, smiling to themselves.

"I can't believe she's eight years old today," Dominic murmured in Ava's ear, when some of the chatter had died down. "Where has the time gone?"

"I've been told that's what happens when you are a parent. Time flies past, and you can't hang onto it. It just goes. Sad, isn't it?"

"I suppose. Happy, too – Daniella is growing into a fine young woman. Oh, and I finally found a governess who is perfect, now that Daniella is well enough to start studying. Shall we interview her together?"

"I would like that," Ava said, flashing a quick, secretive smile at her husband. As always, her heart swelled when she looked at him. As always, his gaze lingered on her as if it were stuck, as if he *couldn't* look away. A slow smile spread over his face, and he opened his mouth to speak.

Whatever he was going to say was unfortunately lost, because Daniella chose that moment to carefully hand Frederick back over to his mother, and announce, "I like babies very much. Papa, Ava, if *you* two had a baby, I should be very pleased. I would like another little brother, or another little sister. Either will do quite well."

The adults burst into incredulous laughter, and Ava shook her head.

"I'm glad you're pleased," Ava said, smiling. "I think it's a little more complicated than simply *wishing* for a little brother or sister, you know."

Daniella shrugged, disgruntled. She turned to say something to Beverley, and Ava glanced back at Dominic.

"Shall we tell her?" Ava murmured, and Dominic chuckled.

"Let's leave it a little while longer. Wait until we're sure."

"You're right, of course."

He lifted her gloved hand to his lips, holding her gaze.

"Of course I'm right. I'm always right, my dear Lady Thame."

She rolled her eyes. "Oh, you are insufferable."

"So I've been told."

Extended Epilogue

Four Years Later

The previous year had been a remarkably mild winter, and it seemed as if Nature was hurrying to make up for that now.

"We're going to be snowed in for a while," Dominic remarked to nobody in particular. Their youngest child, Dorothy, was barely two years old, and currently was asleep in his arms. Behind him was an idyllic scene of domestic bliss.

Idyllic, that is, if a person did not look too closely at the details. For example, if one ignored the fact that Maria was trying to bite her brother James' head, while a ferocious Daniella attempted to separate them. Steven, rather sensibly, had taken his book and retreated to the window seat to read it. Ava was lounging on the sofa, watching her children squabble with a mixture of resignation and amusement.

Dominic turned back from the snow falling thickly past the window and lifted his eyebrows.

"Should we separate them?" he asked, nodding at Maria and James. At three years old, James was already as large as his older sister and more than capable of holding his ground.

"I think they'll sort it out themselves," Ava said, yawning and sitting up. "Come, have some champagne. It's delicious. It's from Beverley, since she, Jason, and Frederick can't make it for Christmastide this year."

Dominic carefully set down the still-sleeping Dorothy on another sofa and took his place beside his wife. Ava curled up beside him, pouring two generous glasses of champagne. As had been their usual custom for the past few years, most of the servants were given time off at Christmas, aside from just the day itself. They rarely bothered with a big celebration, and it made it easier to pull back and enjoy some family time. With Steven at school, Maria just beginning her lessons, and Daniella deep in her studies, it often felt as though the family were not often together.

Ava shifted around, resting her cheek on Dominic's shoulder, and closed her eyes.

"I don't mind that we're snowed in," she said sleepily. "I like it, actually. There's no pressure to pay calls, no worries about being asked to dine out constantly. We can spend time together, with our children. I like this."

Dominic wound an arm around her shoulders, pulling her closer still, and pressed a kiss to her forehead.

"Doesn't it seem strange," he said, in a low voice so that the children wouldn't hear, "That our marriage started as a business arrangement?"

They hadn't, of course, told the children that their parents had married out of mercenary motivations. Half of Society had guessed, and as the children got older, it was likely that they would hear it from somebody else. Perhaps, perhaps not. Either way, it wasn't a subject Dominic or Ava wanted to start on.

She chuckled, taking a sip of her champagne.

"I can't believe it myself at times," she admitted. "Tell me truthfully – did you fall in love with me before or *after* our wedding?"

He winced. "That's a difficult question, because I was *determined* not to be in love with you beforehand. We'd agreed, hadn't we, that ours would be a rational and well-thought-out marriage. We prided ourselves on being remarkably sensible. I felt a great deal towards you, but I did a good job of convincing myself it was all friendship. And that was not, strictly speaking, a lie. We *were* friends first."

"Which is not to be sniffed at."

"Which is *not* to be sniffed at," he agreed. "It's easier than you'd think to not allow yourself to feel something specific. If I had allowed myself, I would have been madly in love with you before the wedding. But as things stand, I think my falling in love with you was a gradual thing. What about you?"

Ava considered, sipping her champagne. Dominic waited patiently for her to finish. It was pleasant not to feel their conversations rushed or listened to. It was good to simply be themselves.

"I think so, too," Ava said at last. "A gradual business. It felt... it felt natural. I didn't want you to feel that you'd been trapped into something, or even tricked into marriage. That happens too often in our world."

He sighed. "I know, and it's a pity. I hope that when our girls come to look about them for husbands, they won't feel obliged to *trick* anybody, or *catch* a husband. The world is changing, and I hope that we are changing with it."

On cue, Daniella got up, dusting off her knees with the newfound grace which signalled her trudge towards womanhood. Already, it was hard to see the sullen, anxious child she had been in her face. The changes were for the better.

She approached Ava and Dominic with a faint, nervous smile.

"Papa, Ava, I wonder if I might have a sip of champagne?"

Dominic choked on his own champagne.

"I think not, dear," Ava said levelly. "Not for a few years, at least. You are rather young, and this champagne is very strong."

"But I'm sure I could just have a little."

"I think not," Dominic choked. "Besides, you wouldn't like it."

She pouted. "But how am I to know if I don't *try* it?"

They all laughed at that and the atmosphere was filled with love and laughter. Ava and Dominic looked at each other silently relishing the life that they trod together and willing to embrace what would follow.

The End

Printed in Great Britain
by Amazon

36972438R00106